KENTUCKY KOMODO DRAGONS

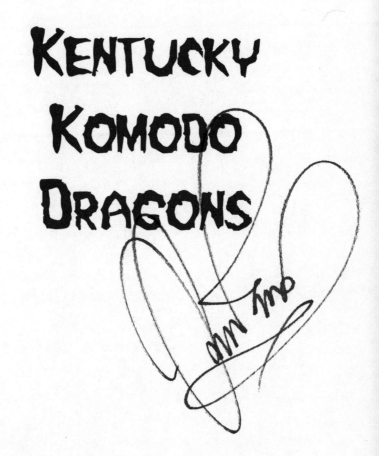

"Dude, your books are the coolest. I used to think reading was boring, but your books aren't! Write faster!"

-Greg G., age 9, Alaska

"I got seven of your books for my birthday. That was last month, and I've read all of them. I can't wait to get more!"

-Jon L., age 12, Nevada

"My sister used to read your books to me, and I thought they were cool. Now, I read them on my own, and I LOVE them!"

-Javon E., age 10, Illinois

"My first book I read was MISSOURI MADHOUSE. It was funny, cool, and scary. Not too scary, but just right."

-Alissa M., age 11, Michigan

"My dad and I read WICKED VELOCIRAPTORS OF WEST VIRGINIA. We both loved it, which is great, because my dad just bought me four more of your books!"

-Derek S., age 8, Florida

"MISSISSIPPI MEGALODON is the best book in the world. How did you come up with that book? It scared the heck out of me. I don't think I'll ever go swimming again."

-Dani M., age 10, Mississippi

"My friends and I love your books so much that we formed an American Chillers book club. We meet every week and make bookmarks and posters. You can come anytime, if you want. Your books are the coolest in the world!"

-Carter F., age 11, Indiana

"I don't know what it is about your books, but they're the only ones I read. They're so good, I've read some of them twice!"

-Gabe L., age 9, New York

"All my friends were reading your books, and I didn't know what the big deal was, until I read one. Now, I love them, too!"

-Jessica O., age 8, Nebraska

"If you make movies about your books, can I be in them? I don't even want any money or nothing."

-Alex F., age 9, Kentucky

"My grandma bought me some of your books at your store, Chillermania. I had never read any of them before, but now I can't stop reading them!"

-Andrew R., age 11, Maine

"I have read every single American Chillers book except MISSISSIPPI MEGALODON. You write great books!"

-Zachary R., age 9, Michigan

"I love to read your books at night, under the covers, with a flashlight. I get really creeped out!"

-Britney., age 10, Louisiana

Got something cool to say about Johnathan Rand's books? Let us know, and we might publish it right here! Send your short blurb to:
Chiller Blurbs
281 Cool Blurbs Ave.
Topinabee, MI 49791

Other books by Johnathan Rand:

#27: Kentucky Komodo Dragons

Johnathan Rand

An AudioCraft Publishing, Inc. book

Book storage and warehouses provided by Chillermania!©
Indian River, Michigan

Warehouse security provided by:
Lily Munster and Scooby-Boo

American Chillers #27: Kentucky Komodo Dragons
ISBN 13-digit: 978-1-893699-90-8

Librarians/Media Specialists:
PCIP/MARC records available **free of charge** at
www.americanchillers.com

Cover illustration by Dwayne Harris
Cover layout and design by Sue Harring

Printed in USA

KENTUCKY
KOMODO
DRAGONS

VISIT CHILLERMANIA!

WORLD HEADQUARTERS FOR BOOKS BY JOHNATHAN RAND!

Yooperland

Indian River

Alpena

Traverse City

MICHIGAN

CHILLERMANIA!

Mt. Pleasant

Bay City

*I-75 Exit 313
then south
1 mile!*

Grand Rapids

Lansing

Detroit

Kalamazoo

Visit the HOME for books by Johnathan Rand! Featuring books, hats, shirts, bookmarks and other cool stuff not available anywhere else in the world! Plus, watch the American Chillers website for news of special events and signings at *CHILLERMANIA!* with author Johnathan Rand! Located in northern lower Michigan, on I-75! Take exit 313 . . . then south 1 mile! For more info, call (231) 238-0338. And be afraid! Be veeeery afraaaaaaiiiid . . . .

1

"Are you ready yet?" I called out down the hall. My sister, Jillian, was still in her room. We had planned on going for a hike in the woods, but she couldn't decide what shirt to wear. She kept changing from one to another. If she kept it up, we'd never get out of the house.

"Just a second, Jason," she said, her voice muffled from behind her closed bedroom door.

"You said that ten minutes ago," I said impatiently. "Make up your mind."

"Hold your horses," Jillian replied.

I sighed. "I'll be on the back porch. We don't have all day, you know."

"No, you don't," Mom called out from her office. "Make sure you're home by noon."

Mom works out of our house in what used to be a guest bedroom. When she started her own business, she turned it into an office. And she stays pretty busy because her phone is always ringing, and she's always tapping away at her computer.

I strode across the living room to her office door. Mom sat at her desk, in front of a computer monitor. She had a telephone headset on, so she could talk to customers while leaving her hands free to type.

"We will, Mom," I said.

Mom smiled. "And stay out of the mud today," she warned.

I smiled meekly and rolled my eyes. The last time I'd gone hiking, it was after a heavy rain. I wound up getting all muddy near a small pond while trying to catch frogs. Mom wasn't very happy when I got home, all soaked and dirty like I was.

Jillian came out of her bedroom. She wore blue jeans and a bright red T-shirt, the color of a fire extinguisher. It had a multi-colored sequined unicorn on the front.

"That's the same shirt you had on ten minutes ago," I said.

"I decided I liked it best," she said smartly.

I frowned and shook my head. "See ya, Mom," I

said, backing away from her office door.

"Bye, Mom," Jillian said.

"Have fun," Mom replied, just as her phone rang. "Don't forget: be home for lunch."

"We will," I said.

Jillian and I walked across the living room, through the kitchen, and out the back door, where we were plastered by a wave of heat. We live in Paducah, Kentucky, which is a city on the western side of the state. It was July, which is a month that gets pretty hot in Kentucky. Just to the north of us is the Ohio River and the state of Illinois. It's kind of weird to think that if we drove just a few miles, we would be in an entirely different state.

And where we live is really cool. There are several other homes on Creekview Drive, and behind our house is a big forest. Jillian and I built a bunch of forts in the woods. Once in a while, Katrina Holland joins us. She lives a few houses away, and she and my sister are best friends.

There's an old story that somewhere in the woods behind our house is an old, forgotten graveyard. It's supposed to be overgrown with trees and weeds, and it's hard to find. In fact, no one has found it for years. There is only one picture of it, and it hangs at the Paducah Historical Museum. Jillian and I have looked for the graveyard a lot, but we've never found it. Still, there's always a chance we might, so we go exploring often. That, of course, was our reason for our hike today: we've always wanted to find the graveyard.

But so far? No luck. There are trails that crisscross through the woods, but we've never found the graveyard. And we don't always follow the trails. Sometimes, we head into the woods to explore on our own. We've been all over the forest, but we still haven't found any sign of the old graveyard.

But what's really cool is that on our hikes, we see all sorts of animals we don't see in the city. Opossums, raccoons, deer, skunks, squirrels, rabbits, and all kinds of birds. The forest behind our house is like one gigantic park, just for us. Lots of animals . . . but no graveyard. At least, not that we could find.

Today, however, we were going to find something that should never have existed. Certainly not in Kentucky, or even in the United States, for that matter.

We strode across the backyard and onto the trail that led into the woods. Above, the sun hung like a lemony ball of fire in front of a blue curtain. It was a hot day already; it was only going to get hotter.

We had hiked for about five minutes along the trail when Jillian suddenly stopped. She was looking ahead, trying to peer through the dense foliage. The terrain around

14

us was thick with trees and shrubs.

"What?" I asked, wiping a thin film of sweat from my forehead. "What did you see? A deer?"

"No," she said. "It was smaller." She pointed. "It's in that tree, right over there. But it's not a bird. Something moved, but I don't know what it is."

I tilted my head to the side, trying to see what she had spotted. I didn't see anything besides trees and branches.

"Probably just a squirrel," I said. "Let's keep going."

We continued on. Branches and tall grass licked at our pant legs like snake tongues. A mosquito buzzed by my ear, and I swatted it away. A small bird chirped and flitted by, lighting on a branch where it continued to chirp.

And when we reached the tree Jillian had pointed to, we heard a noise. It startled us, and we stopped walking and looked up.

Jillian shrieked.

I gasped and jumped back. I looked up . . . and into the face of a monster.

Now, when I say monster, I mean *monster*. Not a monster like Godzilla or anything. What we were seeing was much smaller.

But it was a monster . . . of some sort.

He was about eighteen inches long, and, most obviously, some type of lizard. His skin was leathery, speckled with green, brown, and black markings. His eyes were menacing and sinister, with black pupils ringed with gold. His claws were long and curled, and they looked razor-sharp.

And he was hissing at us! His mouth was open, and we could see his teeth—tiny, but very, very sharp—and a tongue that lashed out like a whip.

Jillian took another step back. "What in the world is that?" she asked.

"It's what you look like in the morning," I replied.

"It's what you look like all the time," Jillian snapped back. "But really . . . what *is* that thing?"

"I don't know," I replied. "Some sort of lizard, I guess."

"We don't have lizards that big around here," she said. "All we have are those little tiny ones that jet around like little rockets with four legs."

"And those other striped ones," I replied. "I think they're called 'skinks.'"

We continued staring at the monster-lizard in the tree. Although we were much bigger than he was, he didn't seem the least bit afraid of us. In fact, he looked like he was mad, like he was protecting his tree. He certainly didn't look like he was going to run from us like most lizards did.

"It must be some sort of rare, endangered species," Jillian said. "I wish we had a camera."

"Maybe he was someone's pet that got away," I said.

"Or," Jillian said, "maybe he escaped from a zoo. Lots of zoos have lizards."

"Or even a pet store," I replied. "We should check the pet stores to see if any of them are missing a hissing

18

lizard."

We were sure there was a logical explanation as to where the creature came from. A lost pet, a zoo, or a pet store seemed . . . well . . . logical.

The truth of the matter was far stranger—and scarier—than we could have ever imagined.

We stared at the strange lizard as he watched us from the tree. Actually, watched isn't the right word. It seemed like he was threatening us more than anything. He was only about as long as my arm, but he looked like he could prove he was mighty, too. Even though we were a lot bigger than he was, I didn't think it would be a good idea to pick a fight with him.

"Let's leave him alone," I said. "We can go to the library and see if we can find him in a book about Kentucky reptiles."

We backed away and made a wide circle around the tree. The lizard watched us warily, but he didn't come after us.

As we hiked, I kept my eyes peeled. I really wanted to find that old, abandoned graveyard, but I couldn't get that silly monster-lizard out of my mind. In fact, that's how I thought of the creature: monster-lizard. He was so unlike any other lizard I'd ever seen. Certainly much bigger, except for the ones I'd seen on television and in zoos. When I was in first grade, we went on a field trip to a zoo, and I saw a Gila monster, which is the only venomous lizard that's native to the United States. They grow to be about two feet long. They can't move very fast, so they're not really a danger to humans, unless someone is intentionally trying to catch them. Then, they'll bite. However, they only live in the southeastern part of the United States, and there aren't very many of them left.

But what we'd seen in the tree wasn't a Gila monster, and it drove me crazy trying to think of what he could be. Certainly not a chameleon or a salamander or a skink.

Weird. Just plain weird.

I looked at my watch. "We should be getting back," I said to Jillian. "Mom wants us home for lunch."

"We'll just have to keep looking," Jillian said. "That old graveyard isn't going to go anywhere."

"Yeah, maybe," I replied. "I might come out after

lunch and look for it."

But there was something I wanted to do first, before we went on another hike in search of the old graveyard. I was going to find out what that monster-lizard was. Then, maybe I could find him again and catch him.

Then again, maybe the thing was dangerous. If he was missing from a zoo or a pet store, there was a good chance he was from another country. Maybe the creature was venomous, like the Gila monster. Maybe he was vicious and mean and bit people.

And that's exactly what I was thinking, hiking through the forest, on our way home . . . when a sharp pain pierced my lower leg!

The pain in my lower leg surprised me so much that I stumbled forward and nearly fell. I was sure the creature we'd seen in the tree had attacked me. I turned and scrambled away, ready to face the charging lizard . . . and got the surprise of my life.

"Gotcha!" Katrina Holland said as she got up from her hiding place. She had been crouching behind a tree, beneath a tree branch, waiting for us.

"You!" I exclaimed. "I'll get you back for that!"

"Fat chance," Katrina said with a smile as wide as the Ohio River. "You should have seen your face! You looked like you were doomed!"

That's a word Katrina is always saying: doomed. Whenever something goes wrong, or is about to go wrong, she uses that word.

Doomed.

And she says it all the time.

"How did you know we were coming?" I asked. I was a little mad, but I had to admit: she'd scared me good. In that sense, it was kind of funny, thinking I'd been attacked by a monster-lizard. I certainly hadn't expected anyone to be hiding behind a tree in the woods.

"Your mom told me you went for a hike," Katrina said, getting to her feet. She had leaves tangled in her black hair, and she pulled them out and let them fall to the ground. "I didn't know if I'd find you or not, but I thought I'd give it a try. Did you find the old graveyard?"

Jillian and I shook our heads. "Not today," my sister said. "I'm beginning to think this whole thing is just a wild goose chase."

"It's out there somewhere," Katrina said, placing her hands on her hips and looking into the forest. "My dad said he found it when he was little. But that was a long time ago, and he doesn't remember where he found it."

"We did find something pretty strange," I said. "A lizard of some sort."

"Big deal," Katrina said with a shrug. "There are

26

lizards all over the place. I saw one on my back porch this morning."

I shook my head. "Not like this one. This one was a lot bigger than the ones we usually see." I explained to Katrina what it looked like, and I spread my hands out to show her how big the creature was. She listened intently, puzzled.

"I've never seen a lizard like that around here before," she said.

We followed the trail home. It was just before noon when we got back, and the three of us were sweating in the late morning sun. Katrina and Jillian made plans to meet after lunch. Katrina's family has a pool in their backyard, and she and Jillian were going to hang out there for a while and cool off in the water.

"You can come, too," Katrina said to me.

I shook my head. "No thanks. I'm going to see if I can find out more about that lizard we found."

During lunch, Jillian and I described the lizard to Mom. She said she'd never seen anything like that before. Not in Kentucky, anyway.

"It was really bizarre looking," Jillian said. "He hissed at us."

"Very strange," Mom said.

Jillian finished her sandwich. "I'm going to put on

27

my swimsuit and go to Katrina's," she said. "We're going to hang out by the pool."

"It's a good day for that," Mom said. "It's going to be hot this afternoon. Thank goodness we have air conditioning."

Jillian got up and went to her room, and I continued telling Mom about the lizard.

"Why don't you use the computer in my office and see if you can find him on the Internet?" she said.

My eyes widened. "That's a great idea!" I replied.

I finished my sandwich, gulped down a glass of lemonade, and hurried into her office.

"Don't touch anything but the computer," Mom called out from the kitchen.

"I won't," I hollered back as I sat at her desk. Mom is a neat freak, and she can't stand it if one thing is out of place . . . especially in her office.

I heard Jillian's bedroom door open. "See ya later, Mom," she said.

"Have fun," Mom replied. Then, I heard the front door open and close.

Seated in front of Mom's computer, I went to a search engine and typed in the words 'lizard,' and 'Kentucky.' Tons of sites came up. I browsed the images, but I didn't see any lizard that looked like the one we saw in the forest. The ones in the pictures were smaller, maybe five or six inches long. I recognized a few of them, as I'd seen them before.

So, I tried another search, this time simply typing in the word 'lizard.' Twenty-one million, nine hundred results were returned! I'd be searching through pictures for hours, if not days!

I quickly scanned the first few pages of images, but I didn't see any lizard that looked like the one we'd spotted. I was about to give up, but I clicked on one more page.

And there it was!

I pulled my hands away from the computer keyboard, and stared. I was looking at the exact lizard that we'd found in the tree. It was unmistakable. I was stunned . . . especially when I saw what kind of lizard it was.

"Mom!" I called out excitedly. My eyes never left the image on the screen. *"Mom! Come here! You've got to see this!"*

"Give me just a minute," Mom called out from the kitchen. "What did you find?" I could hear cupboard doors opening and closing as she put dishes away.

"You're not going to believe it!" I replied. "It's not a lizard . . . it's a dragon!"

"A dragon?" Mom said as she appeared in the doorway.

I pointed at the computer monitor and turned to look up at her. "This is it, right here!" I said, tapping the screen lightly.

Mom moved closer and leaned down. "A baby Komodo dragon?" she said suspiciously. "Are you sure?"

"That's exactly what we saw," I replied. "That's what it is! A baby Komodo dragon!"

"But they don't live in Kentucky, do they?" Mom asked.

My eyes darted rapidly back and forth as I scanned the details on the web page. "No," I replied. "It says here that they don't even live in the United States, except in zoos."

"I wonder what a baby Komodo dragon is doing in Paducah," Mom wondered aloud.

I shook my head. I was puzzled, too, and I shrugged. "You've got me," I replied. "Maybe he escaped from a zoo." I looked up at her. "Do you need your computer right now?"

"Not just yet," Mom said, glancing at her watch, "but I've got to get back to work soon."

Mom went back into the kitchen, and I continued to read about Komodo dragons. Turns out, they aren't really 'dragons,' but lizards, just as I'd suspected. Baby Komodo dragons climb trees, where they are safe from predators. But as they grow, they get too big and heavy to climb trees. In fact, Komodo dragons can grow to ten feet in length, and weigh over three hundred pounds! Komodo dragons are the largest living species of lizard in the world.

But here's the weird part: they only live in Indonesia, which is thousands and thousands of miles from Kentucky.

How did a Komodo dragon get to Paducah, Kentucky? I wondered. The most obvious answers, of course, were the ones we'd already come up with. Either the reptile was someone's pet that got away, or it escaped from a zoo . . . which seemed the most likely answer, as Komodo dragons are protected under government law, and people aren't allowed to keep them. That's what I read on the website, anyway.

So, what zoo? I wondered. We don't have a zoo in Paducah. There's one in Louisville, but that's a long ways away.

And right then, I had another idea. Now that I'd found out what the creature really was, I began to hatch a plan. A plan . . . to catch him.

My mind spun. *I'll be famous!* I thought. I'll catch him, and then I'll call the newspaper and television stations!

I was so excited that I shot up from the chair and raced to my bedroom, thinking about what I would need to catch the baby Komodo dragon. I didn't read anything more about the lizard; I just wanted to catch him and show him off. Sure, I'd probably have to give him to a zoo or somewhere else where he'd be safe. But that was okay. Maybe they would even name him after me!

Jason, the Komodo dragon.

Very cool.

But, as I was about to find out, I should have read more about Komodo dragons. I read only a little bit about them, and I didn't know what they ate, I didn't know where they slept. I didn't know how aggressive, fierce, and dangerous they could be.

But I was going to find out. In fact, I was going to find out more than I'd ever wanted to know . . . the hard way.

I left Mom's office and went into my bedroom. I found my backpack in the closet, and began making a list in my mind of what I thought I would need.

A rope? I thought. No. A rope probably wouldn't do me any good.

But, I would probably want to have a pair of gloves, just in case the thing tried to bite me. The gloves would at least give my hands a little protection.

I left my backpack on the bed and went into the garage, where I found a pair of old gloves Mom uses when she works in the garden. I also found a cloth sack that looked like it would be big enough to hold the lizard. I carried both items back into my bedroom and stuffed them into my backpack. My sunglasses were on my dresser, and I snapped them up and put them on my head.

What else? I wondered. I put my hand on my hips and looked around my bedroom, but I couldn't think of anything else I would need . . . except for a snack or two. I went into the kitchen and found some cookies in the cupboard, along with a bag of potato chips and some beef jerky. In the refrigerator, I found a bottle of water, which would come in handy . . . especially since it was so hot outside.

I carried the items to my bedroom and put them in my backpack. *Now I'm ready*, I thought, slipping my pack over my shoulder. *I'm going to catch me a baby Komodo dragon.*

I strode through the living room and stood at the door of Mom's office. She was busy working at her computer, but paused and turned when I appeared.

"I'm going to see if I can find that thing again," I said. "Maybe I can catch him."

"If you do," Mom warned, "I don't want you bringing it into the house."

"I won't," I replied.

"And don't be gone all afternoon," she added.

"Okay," I said. "See ya later."

I turned, walked through the living room and through the kitchen, and strode out the back door.

The heat from the sun was intense, and I squinted in the bright light. I lowered my sunglasses from my forehead and placed them over my eyes. That helped a lot.

A baby Komodo dragon, I thought. *I wonder where in the world he came from?*

Then, I had another thought: *maybe he's not a Komodo dragon. Maybe he only looks like one.*

No matter. He was still a lizard, and he was cool-looking.

And I was going to catch him.

I hurried across the yard to the trail that wound through the forest, retracing my steps from earlier in the day. All the while, I kept looking around, particularly in low tree branches. After all, there might be more than one baby Komodo dragon.

It wasn't long before I found the very same tree where we'd spotted the lizard. I approached slowly, cautiously, peering up into the branches as I walked. Before I reached the tree, I stopped and slipped my backpack off. I pulled out Mom's gloves and put them on, took a sip of water, then pulled out the cloth bag. I left the backpack on the ground and approached the tree trunk.

If I was a baby Komodo dragon, I wondered, *where*

would I be?

In the tree?

I didn't see him.

I made my way around the tree trunk while I cautiously peered up into the branches. The Komodo dragon would easily blend in with the leaves and limbs, so I looked carefully. He could be three feet in front of me, and would be easy to overlook.

Making my way around the tree, I saw no sign of the lizard. I circled around several more times, but I didn't find the creature. I looked around, into the branches of nearby trees. Still, I found nothing. The only thing that moved was a small bird that lit on a branch for a moment, then quickly chirped and fluttered away.

But I was determined. I knew the reptile had to be around somewhere. All I had to do was find him. I didn't think he could have gone far, but he was probably very good at hiding.

Thirty minutes went by. Then, an hour. I searched high and low, all around the area, in nearby trees, but I found nothing.

After two hours, I still hadn't found the lizard, and I began to get discouraged. I had finally come to the realization I wasn't going to find the creature. The forest was just too big, and there were too many places for him to hide.

I was just about to give up and go home . . . when I heard a twig snap. The sound was far off, but it was loud. I turned, just as I heard another snap.

"Jason!" a voice hollered.

Jillian.

"I'm over here!" I called.

I heard the sound of twigs snapping, and Jillian appeared on the trail. She was wearing shorts and her red T-shirt. Her hair was tied back in a ponytail, and it looked like it was still wet from swimming in the pool.

"There you are," she said. "Did you find the lizard?"

I shook my head. "So far, I haven't seen—"

I stopped speaking, and my entire body stiffened. My skin crawled.

Hiding in the woods, only a few feet from Jillian, was a Komodo dragon.

Not a baby, either. A grown-up, enormous Komodo dragon. I could see only his head, but I knew the thing was probably as big as a car.

"What's the matter?" Jillian asked. "Cat got your tongue?" She was completely unaware of the giant reptile only a short distance from her.

I was just about to shout a warning to her, to tell her to run like crazy, but I didn't have the chance. The giant

Komodo dragon suddenly opened his mouth . . . and charged at my sister!

7

Jillian heard the noise behind her and turned. She let out a wail that was every bit as loud and shrill as a police siren. And maybe the scream frightened the reptile, or maybe it hadn't planned on attacking my sister in the first place. Whatever the reason, the lizard took off in the opposite direction, crashing through the thick brush like an elephant. Soon, the creature was far enough away that we could no longer hear him moving through the woods.

Jillian stood frozen, too afraid to move. I hurried up to her.

"What . . . was . . . that . . . that . . . thing?" she stammered.

"That was a Komodo dragon!" I said. "At least, that's what I think it was." I explained that I'd searched on the Internet and found out the smaller lizard we'd seen was a baby Komodo dragon.

"Well, that must have been the mom or dad," Jillian said. "That thing was gigantic!"

"Let's see if we can find it," I said.

Jillian looked at me like I was out of my mind. In fact, that's just what she said.

"Are you out of your mind?!?!" she said.

I shook my head. "No," I replied. "Let's go see if we can find it. We won't get close to it. That way, we'll get a better look at it, so we can know for sure if it's a Komodo dragon."

"What if he eats us?"

I rolled my eyes. "He's not going to eat us," I said.

But even as I said it, I wasn't all that sure. I'd read that Komodo dragons are carnivores, which means they are meat-eaters. And the one we saw was big. I didn't like the thought of being a lizard lunch.

Still, I was certain that if we kept a safe distance, we'd be fine. Besides: once we knew for sure it was a Komodo dragon, we could report it to the police or someone. We might even be on the television news!

After more coaxing, I finally convinced Jillian to

help me look for the lizard.

"But you have to promise me that we won't get close to it," she said.

"I promise," I said.

Unfortunately, it wasn't a promise I would be able to keep. Oh, it wasn't going to be my fault. I honestly wanted to keep a safe distance away from the Komodo dragon. I didn't realize the Komodo dragon had plans of his own.

I picked up my backpack, slung it over my shoulder, and started in the direction in which we'd seen the Komodo dragon vanish.

"Don't forget to keep an eye out for the little one," I said.

"No way," she said. "I'm keeping my eye out for that big one. I want to make sure I see him before he sees me."

The going was tough, as we were no longer on the trail. The brush grew thick and full, and we had to push much of it out of the way. We tried to be as quiet as we could, but with so many limbs and branches, it was difficult.

And it was hot, too. In no time at all, we'd worked up a sweat. Every so often, we would stop and listen, peering cautiously around us, looking for the Komodo dragon. I was a little nervous, but I didn't want Jillian to know, so I didn't say anything to her.

"I think he's gone," Jillian said. We stopped walking and rested, once again listening and looking for any sign of the Komodo dragon. Blades of sunlight cut through the trees, and the air was moist and smelled punky and leafy-thick. To the right, tall shrubs grew like a wall. To the left, the forest thinned out, giving way to a slight hill covered with long, dry grass the color of wheat. Directly in front of us was a large maple tree.

"He can't be gone," I said. "He's in the forest, somewhere. Let's keep looking."

Just before I was about to turn, I saw something to the left of us—where the hill was—that caught my attention. It was a large hole, a burrow of some sort. Not far from our house, a fox has made a den by digging a hole in the ground. That's what this looked like, only it was a lot bigger. In fact, it looked big enough for a—

Suddenly, Jillian's hand shot out. She pointed at the tree in front of us.

"Jason! Look! There's one right there!"

There was! Perched on a low branch in the maple

tree before us, a baby Komodo dragon sat like a small statue, staring back at us.

"Too cool!" I hissed, opening up the cloth bag in my hands. "I'm going to catch him and take him home!"

"Well," Jillian said, "you'd better hurry up before he gets away."

Cautiously, I approached the tree, not wanting to scare the lizard off. All the while, he watched me warily, but he remained on the branch, unmoving.

Now, I'm pretty good at catching things that move fast: frogs, toads, snakes . . . things like that. I've even caught small fish with my bare hands. The key is patience. You have to take your time, start out slowly and not move very fast, or you'll spook whatever it is you're trying to catch.

Well, I was being patient, moving slowly, not wanting to scare the little Komodo dragon. I wasn't exactly sure how I was going to get him into the bag; I'd figure that out in a moment. The important thing at the time was to get close enough to the creature without him running off.

But Jillian and I were so focused on the baby Komodo dragon we didn't realize a very important fact: something was emerging from the burrow in the hill.

Something enormous . . . .

Although Jillian and I heard the noise at the same time, it was she who turned and realized the danger first. Surprisingly, she didn't scream. She didn't yell or shout or anything like that.

"J . . . Ja . . . Jason?" she stammered. She spoke slowly, and her voice trembled.

"What?" I asked. I could tell something was scaring her, but I remained focused on the baby Komodo dragon in the tree. After all: it might be the only good chance I had to catch him.

"There's . . . there's something coming out of that hole in the ground over there." Her voice was heavy with fear.

"Hold on," I said quietly. "I've got to get this thing in the bag."

Jillian continued speaking, and her voice continued to shake and tremble.

"I think you'd . . . you'd better look *now,*" she said. "And I mean *right now.*"

Without moving too much, my eyes darted to the side. Whatever she was seeing was out of my range of vision, and I slowly turned my head.

When I saw what Jillian was looking at, I quickly forgot about the baby Komodo dragon. In that split second, I realized I had a much bigger problem than catching a small lizard.

Emerging from the burrow, head first, was a giant Komodo dragon! He was using his claws to pull himself out, moving slowly, turning his head from side to side. He was about thirty feet away . . . which, as far as I was concerned, was much too close.

Jillian started to speak again.

"We've got to get—"

"Shhhh!" I hissed, and she fell silent. "Maybe he can't see or hear us!"

I remembered reading that Komodo dragons can't hear very well. They have fairly good eyesight, but they have difficult seeing objects that don't move. I hoped if we stayed very still and didn't make any loud sounds, the enormous lizard wouldn't know we were there.

And although I didn't know how fast Komodo dragons could move, I was hoping we would be able to outrun him, if we had to. I'd read that, typically, Komodo dragons tend to lay in wait, ambushing their prey when it wandered by. Maybe they couldn't move very fast, but had only short bursts of speed for taking down their next meal.

Let's just hope he doesn't want us for his lunch, I thought.

My heart was racing, and I'd forgotten all about the baby Komodo dragon in the tree. Both excitement and terror pumped through my veins. Excitement, because it really was a thrill to see the giant reptile. Terror, because we were so very close to the thing . . . and we had no idea what he was capable of.

When the lizard had completely emerged from the burrow, he stopped. Then, he slowly raised his head. His tongue lapped out, like he was licking the air. I was amazed at how big he was.

The creature turned his head from side to side.

Then, he drew his head back.

His tongue lapped out again.

Slowly, his head turned . . . until he was looking

51

right at us.

My heart beat faster. A film of perspiration had formed on my forehead, and a bead of sweat rolled down my nose. My skin was hot and clammy.

Could he see us? I wondered. *Does he know we're here? Can he smell us?*

My answer came when the giant Komodo dragon suddenly lurched forward . . . and attacked.

In times like this—when you're being attacked by a giant monster—there's not a lot of time to think. Of course, I'd never been attacked by a giant monster before, so I really didn't know what to do.

But I knew this: that thing was coming after us, and if we didn't do something fast, we were going to be his lunch. I didn't know how fast the thing could move, but I wasn't taking any chances.

"Up the tree!" I shouted as I sprang. The baby Komodo dragon that had been sitting on the branch was already gone. I don't think he wanted to hang around, either.

I dropped the cloth bag as I reached the tree.

Thankfully, there were a lot of low branches to grab. Jillian, too, was at the tree in no time, and she grabbed a branch and began to pull herself up. Like me, Jillian is an excellent tree climber . . . which was a good thing for both of us.

I pulled with my arms and looped my right leg over a branch. Behind me, I could hear the huge Komodo dragon raging toward us, with his size and weight snapping twigs and branches as he charged closer.

Now, all of this was happening in a matter of seconds. I didn't have time to think about anything else except climbing up into the tree and hoping Jillian would be able to do the same thing. And let me tell you: I was climbing faster than I've ever climbed in my life! Usually, when I climb a tree, I don't move very fast. I don't want to slip and fall and land on my head or break an arm. But if I fell now, I'd have a lot more to worry about than a bumped noggin or a broken bone.

Jillian was screaming as she climbed, but she was making progress, pulling herself higher and higher. Beneath us, I could hear the Komodo dragon. He'd reached the tree, and I could hear his claws scraping at the trunk, which made me climb even faster. Once, my backpack caught on a small branch, but it didn't slow me down. The tiny branch snapped, but my pack remained on my back.

I hope what I read is right, I thought. *I hope that*

grown-up Komodo dragons are too big and heavy to climb trees. Otherwise, we're history.

Finally, when I thought I was high enough, I looked down. Beneath me was a truly terrifying sight.

The Komodo dragon was at the base of the tree, standing up. He was leaning on the trunk with his front claws. His mouth was open, and his head was swaying from side to side. If I fell now, I would fall right into his powerful jaws.

"That thing is going to eat us!" Jillian shrieked. "I don't want to be a lizard lunch!"

"I don't think he can climb up!" I yelled. *"He's too big!"*

We continued to climb, just to be safe. Quickly, however, it was apparent I was right. The enormous Komodo dragon couldn't climb the tree. If he had been able to, my sister and I would have been lizard food.

Suddenly, we heard a distant shout.

"Hey, you guys! Where are you?!?!"

I recognized Katrina's voice immediately, and I looked through the dense, leafy branches to see if I could see her.

And so did the giant Komodo dragon. He'd heard her shout, and she had attracted his attention. The giant beast dropped to all fours and froze, listening intently.

"Where are you guys?!?!" Katrina shouted again.

"Katrina!" I yelled. *"Don't come any closer! Run home and get help!"*

"What?!?!" she hollered back.

Beneath me, the Komodo dragon's head was bobbing back and forth, listening, trying to gauge where Katrina's voice was coming from.

"Go back!" I hollered. "There's a Komodo dragon that is going to eat you up!"

"Stop kidding around!" Katrina shouted. "Really! Where are you?!?!"

I tried to see her, but it was impossible through all the branches and leaves.

"He's not kidding around!" Jillian shouted. "A monster attacked us!"

Below, the Komodo dragon lowered to the ground and began to move.

Toward the sound of Katrina's voice.

"Where are you guys?" she yelled again. She was getting closer to us, and she had no idea of the danger she was in.

We could no longer see the giant Komodo dragon. He'd stalked off into the woods, hunting for Katrina.

"Katrina!" I shouted. "Please! Go home! Even if you don't believe us about the Komodo dragon, just go home!

Otherwise—"

Katrina interrupted me. "I don't know what you're—"

Her voice stopped. Suddenly, it was followed by a horrifying shriek as she screamed at the very top of her lungs. Then:

"Oh, my gosh! It's a monster! He's after me! I'm doomed! I'm doooooooomed!"

11

I heard a tremendous crashing of branches and a violent snapping of twigs. Katrina screamed once more, and then she fell silent. In fact, there were no other sounds in the forest, except for a few unseen birds chirping in the distance.

Nothing else.

No branches breaking, no leaves cracking, no brush moving.

No Katrina.

"Oh, no!" Jillian gasped. "That thing ate Katrina!"

"Katrina!" I yelled. "Are you all right?!?!"

We listened, but Katrina didn't reply.

"Oh, no!" Jillian repeated. "That thing got her! I just know it!"

"Maybe she was able to run away," I said. "That's why she's not answering."

"Katrina!" Jillian shouted.

We listened. Still, we heard nothing, and I began to realize Jillian might be right: maybe that giant Komodo dragon had eaten Katrina.

The thought was horrifying. I knew I wouldn't like it if a huge monster ate me. You probably wouldn't, either.

"We have to find out," I said, slipping down a branch. A branch hit my forehead, nearly knocking off my sunglasses. I adjusted the frame and continued to climb down.

"Find out?!?!" Jillian exclaimed.

"Yeah," I replied. "Maybe Katrina needs our help. Maybe she didn't get gulped down."

"But what if that thing gets us?" Jillian asked.

"What if he doesn't?" I asked. I tried to sound brave, but I was actually more than just a little afraid. In fact, I was terrified. But Katrina might be in trouble. We might be able to do something to save her . . . if, of course, we weren't already too late.

"Come on," I urged Jillian. "I mean . . . I'll go by myself if I have to, but we have to find out what happened to Katrina."

Jillian began to climb down the tree. "What are we going to do?" she asked as she carefully lowered herself from limb to limb.

I dropped cautiously to the ground, looking for any sign of the giant lizard. It occurred to me the baby Komodo dragon had vanished, too, and I looked up into the tree to see if I could see him. Nope.

Jillian dropped to the ground.

"This way," I said, pointing. "That thing is so big, he's made his own path through the woods. Let's go slow, and be quiet."

Slowly, we set out through the forest, following the trail made by the Komodo dragon. My backpack was rubbing against my shoulder blades, so I slipped it off and carried it in my right hand. Jillian followed right behind me, and every few feet we would stop, look, and listen for any signs of the giant lizard. I wanted to make sure we saw him before he saw us. And although I wanted to call out for Katrina, I didn't want to make any noise that might attract the attention of the reptile.

We stopped at a small hill and looked around.

"She's got to be around here, somewhere," I whispered.

"Not if that thing ate her in one gulp," Jillian

61

replied quietly. "Then, she'll be in his belly."

The thought wasn't a pleasant one. I couldn't imagine being eaten by anything . . . especially a giant Komodo dragon!

Jillian suddenly pointed. "What's that, up there?" she whispered.

I strained to see what she was looking at. At first, I didn't see anything . . . but that was because the Komodo dragon's colors allowed it to blend in with the leaves and branches. It would have been easy to miss him altogether.

"That's him!" I whispered.

The Komodo dragon was facing away, and he hadn't spotted us.

"Do you see Katrina?" Jillian asked.

I shook my head . . . just as the enormous reptile turned. When we saw what he had in his mouth, my heart fell, and a sudden, new wave of horror swept through my body. It was a fear and sadness I'd never experienced before.

A small yellow cloth dangled from the side of the Komodo dragon's mouth, hanging limply from his jaw.

"Oh, no!" Jillian whimpered. "Katrina was wearing a yellow T-shirt! That thing got her! He ate my best friend!"

12

I'm no stranger to trouble. Once, I broke a window with a rock and Mom grounded me for a week. Another time, I hid in my sister's closet, so I could jump out and scare her. It worked, all right, but Jillian freaked out and started crying. Mom got so mad at me that I was grounded again.

But the trouble we were in at the moment was different. It was far worse than any other trouble we'd been in before. Now that we'd realized the giant Komodo dragon was vicious—that he'd actually eaten Katrina Holland—we knew we could easily be next . . . especially if he spotted us.

"Stay . . . perfectly . . . still," I said in a voice just above a whisper, my lips barely moving. The giant lizard was looking in our direction, and I didn't want to move a single inch and risk him spotting us.

We watched as the creature opened his mouth. The torn, yellow cloth that had once been Katrina's T-shirt fell to the ground. Then, the beast's tongue lashed out, licking the air.

I hope he doesn't smell us, I thought. I hope he goes away.

Finally, he began crawling through the forest, away from us. Relief grew inside of me as the creature continued lumbering off. Soon, we could no longer see him. We heard the snapping of twigs and branches for nearly a minute, until those sounds faded completely. Once again, all we could hear were a few birds in the distance. It was like a normal day in the forest, except, of course, for the fact that there was a bloodthirsty monster on the loose.

"Let's get out of here," Jillian said. "Let's get out of here before he comes back."

"We're going to have to cut through the woods," I said. "I don't know where the trail is . . . but I think our house is over that way." I pointed. "Follow me, and be quiet."

"You don't have to tell me to be quiet," Jillian said.

I was still carrying my backpack as we started out, walking through the brush, weaving around trees and tall bushes. It was slow going, because we were trying to be as quiet as possible. Plus, we remained on the lookout for the giant Komodo dragon. My eyes scoured the forest, hoping to catch sight of the creature before he saw us . . . if we saw him at all.

While we walked, I thought about poor Katrina and her last words. She had screamed she was doomed. She had always used that word, usually when it wasn't necessary.

This time, however, she had been right. She was doomed . . . and she would never use that word again.

Doomed.

And I wondered what we would say to her mom and dad. How do you tell parents that their daughter has been eaten by a giant reptile? I doubted they would even believe me, until Katrina didn't show up for dinner. Then, they'd realize she wasn't coming back. They'd realize their daughter had been doomed.

But a lot of other people would be doomed if that creature wasn't caught soon. Jillian and I weren't the only people who hiked in the forest. Others might stumble upon the Komodo dragon and face the same fate as Katrina.

But not if we could help it. I was sure Mom would believe us. Sure, it seemed crazy, but I knew Mom would take us seriously. She'd call the police, and they would be able to help. They would form some sort of fence or barrier all the way around the woods, surrounding the forest. That way, no one could get in, and the Komodo dragon couldn't get out. They might not know what to do right away, but at least people would be safe.

Except, of course, Katrina. For her, it was already too late.

Our problems, however, were going to get worse in two ways: first, after walking for some time, I had to finally admit we were lost. Oh, I knew sooner or later, we'd find our way out and make our way home because the forest really isn't all that big.

But that wasn't the really big problem. The second, really big problem was that we were going to discover there wasn't just one giant Komodo dragon in the forest. There were more. And if we thought what had happened to Katrina was bad, it was nothing compared to what the enormous reptiles would have in store for Jillian and me . . . .

13

After we'd walked for a while and still hadn't found our way out of the woods, we stopped. I took my sunglasses off and wiped the lenses on my shirt to clean them. I put my backpack on and returned the glasses to my face.

"Are we lost?" Jillian asked.

"Not for long," I said, looking around. I was searching for a tall tree, figuring I could climb up near the top. From there, I should be able to see houses and buildings in the distance. It wouldn't be that difficult to find our way out, once we knew which direction to go.

I found a tree—a tall maple with lots of limbs—not far from where we were standing.

"I'll climb up and see which way we have to go," I told Jillian. "We'll be out of the woods and home soon."

"I feel awful about Katrina," she said, and her voice cracked with despair. Katrina had been Jillian's best friend, and now she was gone forever.

She followed me to the maple tree. I grabbed a low branch and began pulling myself up, scurrying up the tree like a monkey. Higher and higher I climbed, and the branches grew smaller and thinner as I neared the top.

Finally, I was high enough so I could see over the tops of other trees. The problem was, I still wasn't high enough to see our neighborhood or any other houses, for that matter. But I did see something else that was interesting: a building in the middle of a field. But it certainly wasn't any ordinary structure. It was gray and cone-shaped and appeared to be made out of metal or steel. I could make out what appeared to be windows and a door. It was weird. It looked like a tin can wigwam. In all the times I'd explored the forest, I'd never seen it before.

What's a strange building like that doing in the middle of the woods? I wondered.

No matter. I was sure there would be someone there. They would have a phone, and we could call for help.

I started down the tree . . . until I saw something else.

Giant Komodo dragons.

Not *one*.

Not *two*.

Three of them.

They were moving slowly, as if hunting for something, ready to attack. In fact, that's what they were doing: stalking their prey.

And that prey happened to be Jillian!

14

"Jillian!" I shouted. I knew the Komodo dragons would hear me, but, by the way it looked, they already knew where Jillian was. All three of them were slinking toward her . . . she just didn't know it.

"What?" Jillian asked as she looked up at me.

"Climb up, quick!" I shouted down to her. "There are three of those things coming toward you!"

That was all I needed to say. Jillian leapt up and grabbed the nearest branch, expertly pulling herself up and off the ground. In no time at all, she was scrambling through the branches, far enough up so the Komodo dragons wouldn't be able to reach her.

Man, I thought. I sure am glad those things don't climb trees.

Jillian climbed up to the branch I was clinging to and held onto it for her life.

"Where are they?" she asked.

I pointed. "Down there. Do you see them?"

Jillian looked where I was pointing. "No," she replied.

"It's because they aren't moving now," I said, "and they're blending in with their surroundings. There are three of them, and they were coming right toward you."

Suddenly, one of them moved by raising its head. It was only a slight motion, but it was all that was needed for my sister to see him.

"Oh, there he is," Jillian said.

"There are two more right next to him," I replied.

"How many are there?" Jillian wondered aloud. "I mean . . . we've already seen a few of them. How many do you think are in the forest?"

I shook my head slowly. "I don't have any idea," I answered. "They're not even supposed to be here. They must have escaped from a zoo or something."

"But there aren't any zoos around here," she said.

I nodded. "I know. But they had to have come from somewhere. We've been through these woods dozens of times, and we've never seen them before. And look."

I pointed over the treetops to the cone-shaped steel building in the middle of the field.

"What is that place?" Jillian asked.

"I've never seen it before," I said. "But there are a lot of places in the forest we haven't explored."

"It seems like a strange place for a house," Jillian said, "if that's what it is."

She was right. Most homes were in subdivisions, along streets,
 or at least somewhere near a road or highway. From what I could see, there didn't appear to be any roads near the structure. It looked strangely out-of-place in the field. Desolate and alone, even.

"If we can make it to that building," I said, "they will probably have a phone. We can call Mom, and she can come and get us."

"What about them?" Jillian asked as she pointed to the three Komodo dragons below.

"We wait," I said. "We wait for them to leave, then we climb down and run to the building. It won't take us more than a few minutes."

The good thing was, I was right. We would make it to the strange-looking building, and it would take us only a couple of minutes.

The bad thing was that we had no idea what we were about to discover. I've heard it said before that the truth is often stranger than fiction. Well, the truth we were about to uncover wasn't just stranger than fiction . . . it was horrifying.

It didn't take long for the Komodo dragons to become bored. They watched us for a few minutes and then became uninterested. They must have realized that while we were in the tree, they couldn't get us, and they got tired of waiting. One of them started to move off, and the other two followed. When we could no longer see them, Jillian spoke.

"Do you think it's safe?" she asked.

"Probably," I said. "But just to be sure, let's wait a few more minutes."

We waited. I was constantly on the lookout for the three Komodo dragons—or any others, for that matter—but I didn't see any. Finally, when I was confident they'd moved on, we began climbing down the tree. I hung on the last branch, in the air, searching our surroundings for any of the creatures, just in case. Not seeing any, I dropped to the ground. Jillian did the same and stumbled, but I grabbed her arm to keep her from falling.

"Let's go," I said, and we started off in the direction of the cone-shaped building. Of course, now that we were on the ground, we could no longer see it. But I had a pretty good idea where it was.

"Try not to make a lot of noise," I said as we hurried through the forest. Branches and twigs cracked and snapped beneath our feet.

"Yeah, right," Jillian said. "We sound like two charging hippos. If there are any of those things around, they're going to hear us, for sure."

"All the more reason for us to get to that building as fast as we can," I said.

"I just hope someone is home," said Jillian. "It's not going to do us any good if nobody is home and we can't use a phone."

Jillian was right, but I was confident someone would be around. Even if there wasn't anyone home, I was sure we'd be able to find someplace safe, where the Komodo dragons couldn't get at us. How I knew this, I don't know. Maybe it was just wishful thinking.

We hurried through the forest until I caught a glimpse of gray through the trees.

"There it is!" I said, pointing. *"It's right up there!"*

We continued on, ducking under branches and around trees. Then, the woods abruptly stopped, opening up to a large clearing.

I stopped, and so did Jillian. We both stared in curiosity and amazement at what we were seeing . . . and we both knew things had just taken another strange, bizarre twist.

16

It wasn't the building that was so strange . . . it was the tall, wire-mesh fence topped with barbed wire that wound all around the edge of the clearing. There were red and white signs posted every few feet. Some said 'KEEP OUT!'; others said 'NO TRESPASSING!' and 'PRIVATE PROPERTY!'

"There sure are a lot of keep out signs," Jillian said.

"I guess somebody really wants to keep people out," I replied, pointing to the barbed wire. "Look at that. If anyone tries to climb over the fence, they'll be torn to ribbons."

We stood quietly, staring. A bird flew from the

forest, over the odd, cone-shaped building, and vanished into the woods on the other side of the clearing. A bug buzzed near my head, and I swatted it away. A gentle breeze whispered through the trees.

"That building is weird-looking," Jillian said. "It looks like an upside-down ice cream cone made out of silver."

My backpack had started rubbing into my shoulder blades again, and I slipped it off. I pulled out my water bottle, took a sip, and gave it to Jillian. After she took a drink, she handed it back, and I returned it to my backpack, carrying it in my left hand. We continued staring.

And I couldn't help but think something was very, very wrong. There was something not right about the building, the fence, and the clearing. Now that we were closer, we could see the structure didn't appear to be a home, after all. It was too rigid, too cold and stale-looking to be someone's house. In fact, it looked more like something out of a science fiction movie. The windows were strange, too. They were round and shiny, like mirrors, and it didn't look like we'd be able to see inside.

"It doesn't look like anyone is around," I said. "Let's follow the fence and see if we can find a driveway or something."

We started walking, following the fence as it wound

around the perimeter of the clearing. I continued looking for anything that would give a clue as to what the building was, but I didn't see anything. There wasn't a clue anywhere, except for the many warning signs posted all along the fence.

"Look at that," I said, pointing. Ahead of us, there was a large tear in the fence, easily big enough for a human to slip through. The mesh wires had been mangled and torn, like they had been hastily cut. The ends of the wires were sharp and pointy, and if we tried to get through, we'd probably get a cut or two.

"What happened there?" Jillian asked.

I shrugged. "Something ripped open the fence," I said, looking around warily, "and I'll bet I know what that something is."

We stared at the large hole, then gazed at our surroundings. I wondered if, at that very moment, there was a giant Komodo dragon hiding in the forest, watching, waiting for the right moment to attack us. I started to get a little nervous, too, but I shook the feeling off.

Don't even think about it, Jason, I told myself. *Just focus on getting home.*

"Look," I said. "There's a gate up there. Come on."

We started walking along the fence again. My backpack was getting heavy, and I was getting tired of carrying it, so I slipped it over my shoulder.

When we reached the gate, we stopped. It was made of thick, rusty metal. There was a heavy chain wrapped around it, with a large, silver combination lock. A winding trail led away from the gate and into the woods.

"The bars are too close together," I said as I inspected the fence. "We won't be able to wiggle through."

I looked around. "Well," I said, "we're not getting in this way. Somebody really wants to keep everyone out."

"It doesn't look like there's anyone around anyway," Jillian said.

High above, the sun cast its stifling heat and bright light upon us. The breeze was gone, and the trees were motionless. I could hear birds chirping in the forest. Suddenly, they stopped. Not one at a time, but all of them at once, like each had been silenced at the exact same time. Even Jillian noticed it.

"That's weird," she said. "All of the birds stopped singing."

We listened, but there was nothing to hear. No leaves rustling, no vehicles in the distance, no hum of an airplane far away. The only thing we could hear was—

Nothing.

And then a feeling began to creep over me. It was like a cold draft drifting over my skin, covering me like a blanket. The hair on my arms stood up, and I broke out in goose bumps, even though the day was hot.

"I'm scared," Jillian said. She was having the same feeling I was.

"There's nothing to be scared about," I said, although I wasn't so sure myself. I pointed. "Let's just follow this trail. I'm sure it will lead us out to a main road, and we'll be able to find our way home. We'll just have to keep an eye out for those things."

"Mom isn't going to believe us," Jillian said.

"Yes, she will," I replied as we started walking along the driveway. "She knows we don't make things up."

"What about the story you told her about your homework?" she asked.

I laughed out loud. One time, I left my homework at school by accident. I made up a big story, telling my mom that flying monkeys took my homework. They chewed it up and ate it, I told her. I was only kidding, of course, and Mom knew it.

"That was just a joke," I said. "Mom knew I was kidding. But she'll know we're not kidding when we tell her about the Komodo dragons."

"What are we going to say to Katrina's parents?" Jillian asked.

By now, the creeping feeling of fear was gone, and

I was suddenly very sad. What had happened to Katrina was awful, and I couldn't help but think that it was all our fault. Or, my fault, anyway. Jillian didn't have much to do with it. If I hadn't been out looking for that baby Komodo dragon, none of this would have happened. Jillian wouldn't have come looking for me, and Katrina wouldn't have come looking for Jillian.

A loud snapping sound to the left caught our attention, and we stopped walking. We both turned.

"What was that?" Jillian whispered.

I shook my head, but I didn't say anything.

Then, we heard another snap and a crunching sound.

A branch moved, ever so slightly, bobbing back and forth. Something caused it to move. Then, it was still.

"I have a really bad feeling about this," Jillian whispered.

I did, too . . . but I didn't say anything.

"Let's keep going," Jillian said quietly. "If we don't move too—"

A sudden, loud crunch in the forest stopped my sister in mid-sentence, and we both jumped. An enormous head—the head of a giant Komodo dragon—appeared through the branches. He was looking right at us.

Then, another lizard appeared ahead of us on the trail, blocking our way.

Behind us, thirty feet away, was the gate.

It was locked.

It was then

I realized that what happened to Katrina was about to happen to us. I hated to admit it, but the time had come. It was the end of the road for Jillian and me.

We were *doomed.*

17

We weren't surrounded, but it didn't matter. With the gate behind us locked, and the Komodo dragons in front of us, we were trapped. There was nowhere we could go, and I doubted we would be able to outrun the giant lizards. Maybe a deer or a dog could, but not two kids. After all: Katrina hadn't been able to outrun them.

And we couldn't climb the fence or the gate because of the barbed wire.

Things looked pretty grim.

Both of the giant lizards started toward us at the same time. Their heads were low, swinging from side to side. Their snake like tongues lapped at the air. They looked menacing and mean, like giant alligators, but with longer legs.

Suddenly, a thought came to mind, and I remembered the hole in the fence we'd discovered. It was on the other side of the yard, but we might be able to reach it . . . if we didn't waste a single second. Of course, we might get cut by the sharp ends of the fence, but it seemed a whole lot better than being chomped in two by a man-eating lizard!

"Through the fence!" I shouted, and we spun around and started running. *"We can wiggle through the hole in the fence!"*

"But what if they can wiggle through, too?!?!" Jillian shrieked.

"We don't have anywhere else to go!" I shouted. And we didn't. We couldn't run into the woods because we would be slowed down by the trees and brush. The Komodo dragons would easily be able to catch up to us. Our only chance would be to make it through the fence and hope that we might be able to find a way into the building. Maybe someone was inside after all. Maybe the door was open, and we could go inside if we had to. It was a long shot, but it was the only chance we had.

Our sneakers pounded the hard packed dirt. My backpack, I realized, was slowing me down, so I let it slip off of my back and fall to the ground. I didn't even take the time to look behind me, as I was focused only on the hole in the fence. Jillian was by my side, and we were running faster than we've ever run in our lives.

When we made it to the hole in the fence, I was running so fast I couldn't stop. I bounced off the tightly-bound wires, and Jillian ran into me. Instantly, I grabbed the two sides of the fence that had been torn and pulled them apart, making the hole wider.

"Go!" I shouted to my sister. "Be careful! Try not to get cut!" Jillian ducked down and easily slipped through. I was right behind her. I tried to hold the fence apart, but my shirt caught on one of the wires. I heard a tear as the cloth ripped, but I didn't care. I was just glad it wasn't my skin, and I slipped through without injury.

I turned around to see both of the giant Komodo dragons. They were close—only a few feet from the fence—but they had stopped and weren't coming any closer. In fact, they paced slowly from side to side, warily watching the fence, as if they were afraid of it. And thankfully, they didn't attempt to come through the hole.

Strange.

We backed away from the fence and toward the cone-shaped building. Jillian had described it perfectly: it really did look like an upside-down ice cream cone.

The Komodo dragons began to circle around the fence, but they didn't get any closer. It was obvious they wanted to get to us, but they couldn't. And, for whatever reason, they wouldn't go through the hole in the fence.

We reached the strange looking building, which towered above us like a pointed skyscraper. There was a large, metal door at the middle of the building. I pounded on it and waited, hoping to hear someone inside, hoping the door would open. When no one answered, I pounded again.

"I don't think anyone's home," Jillian said.

"Well, at least we're safe, I think," I replied. "Those things don't like the fence. It's like they're afraid of it or something."

"That's fine with me," Jillian said. "I don't want them anywhere near me."

I looked for a doorknob, but I didn't find one. That's really strange, I thought. Whoever heard of a door without a doorknob?

"Look," Jillian said. "They're going away."

I turned around. The two Komodo dragons were slinking off into the forest. Now that they hadn't been able to snag us for lunch, they were off to search for something else to eat.

"Well, at least we know we're safe here," I said. "As long as those things don't come through the fence, we'll be fine."

"And when we don't go home for dinner," Jillian said, "Mom will come looking for us."

"That's another problem," I said. "Mom has no idea those things are out there. If she comes to look for us, she's going to wind up just like Katrina."

"We can't let that happen!" Jillian said, shocked. "It's bad enough that I just lost my best friend! We can't let the same thing happen to Mom!"

"The only thing we can do is try to leave again," I said. "We could follow that trail, like we were doing. That's our way out . . . but we might run into more of those Komodo dragons."

"This isn't fair!" Jillian pouted.

"It doesn't matter whether it's fair or not," I said. "It's reality. It's what's happening, and we just have to deal with it."

"I don't like this reality," Jillian said.

"Yeah, well a lot of people don't like their reality, but they're stuck with it, just like us. Besides: if you think you have it bad, just think about how bad it was for Katrina."

I shouldn't have said that. I didn't say it to be mean, but I guess it came out that way. Tears formed in Jillian's eyes.

"She was my best friend," she said. "We should have done something to help her."

"We did everything we could," I said. "Now, we have to think about ourselves. We can't think back about what we could have done. We need to think about how we're going to get home alive."

Suddenly, a piercing shriek echoed through the forest. It was far off, but it was the sound of a girl screaming.

Jillian's eyes widened and I thought they were going to pop out of her head. She grabbed my arm hard, causing me to wince in pain.

"That's Katrina!" she shouted. "I'd know her scream anywhere!"

"It can't be!" I said.

"It is!" Jillian replied. "Somehow, she's alive! She needs help! I didn't help her before, but now I have another chance!"

Without saying anything more, she let go of my arm and started running to the hole in the fence.

"Jillian!" I shouted. "Wait!"

"I'm not waiting another second!" Jillian shouted. "That's Katrina, and I'm going to help her!"

Somehow, Katrina was still alive. Sure, I wanted to help her . . . but we needed to think about what we could do.

We needed a plan of some sort.

But Jillian wasn't thinking that way. She was racing to Katrina's aid, and she had no idea what kind of trouble she was about to get into.

I had no choice but to follow Jillian. Oh, I didn't want to. I didn't want to go back into the forest, not with those freaky, man-eating lizards out there.

But I couldn't let my sister go alone. She was going to help Katrina, and she was willing to risk her own life to do it. And I wasn't about to let anything happen to my sister if I could help it. After all: if something happened to Jillian, I wouldn't have anyone to play practical jokes on.

I raced to the fence and slipped through the hole. Jillian had just vanished into the forest and was calling to Katrina, telling her to keep shouting, so she'd be able to follow the sound of her voice and find her. Although I couldn't see Jillian, she was making enough noise charging through the forest that all I had to do was follow the sounds. Of course, that would mean the Komodo dragons would be able to hear her, too . . . if there were any nearby. It was too late to tell her to be quiet. She was on a mission to help Katrina, and she wasn't thinking about giant Komodo dragons. She was thinking only about her friend.

While I charged through the forest after my sister, I tried to be on the lookout for more Komodo dragons. They could be anywhere, and the fact that they blended in with their surroundings made me nervous. I could be five feet from one of them and not even see the thing. Then, of course, it would be too late.

I caught a glimpse of my sister up ahead. "Jillian!" I shouted. "Wait for me!"

Jillian ignored me. Instead, she called out to Katrina.

"Katrina!" she shouted. "Where are you?!?!"

"I'm here!" Katrina's voice echoed through the woods. "I'm up in a tree!"

"I can see you!" Jillian shouted.

"One of those things chased me!" Katrina wailed.

"I know!" Jillian shouted back. "They chased us, too!"

By now, I had reached Jillian. We were at the base of a large oak tree. High above, Katrina was clinging tightly to a thick, sturdy branch.

I looked around, ready to climb up the tree if I had to.

"Can you see any of them from up there?" Jillian shouted.

"No," Katrina replied. "The one that chased me took off in a hurry. He almost got me!"

"Come down and let's get out of here," I said. "We're sitting ducks, here in the woods. There's a building not far away, and the lizards won't go near it. We'll be safe if we can make it back there."

Katrina slipped in between, over, under, and around branches, carefully making her way down the tree and to the ground.

"Look at what one of them did to my shirt!" Katrina exclaimed. She turned around. A large chunk of the back of her T-shirt was missing, torn away by the powerful jaws of the Komodo dragon.

"You're lucky it was just your shirt," I said. "We heard you scream and thought you got eaten up."

"What are they?" she asked.

"Komodo dragons," I replied. "We saw a baby lizard earlier today, and I went home and looked it up on my mom's computer."

"Komodo dragons?" Katrina asked.

"In Kentucky? They're not supposed to live here."

"Maybe not, but they're here," I said.

"And they want to eat us," Jillian said with a shudder.

"Let's get back to that building," I said, and I started walking. "For some reason, those things are afraid of the building or the fence."

"I'm so glad you're alive," Jillian said, and she gave Katrina a hug. "I thought you were gone forever."

"Hey, I'm glad, too," Katrina said. "But I'm mad at that thing for ripping my shirt. I just got it last week!"

We hurried through the forest, making our way back to the building. The fence soon came into view, then the clearing and the building.

"That thing is weird-looking," Katrina said. "It's like a metal teepee."

Suddenly, there was a heavy crashing of branches only a few feet away . . . and I knew in an instant we wouldn't make it to the fence . . . .

19

When the noise exploded in the branches and brush nearby, I immediately assumed we were being attacked by a Komodo dragon.

I was wrong, and never in my life had I been so happy to be wrong. It wasn't a Komodo dragon that had created the noise . . . it was a deer! She must have been sleeping, and we had surprised her. She bounded off into the woods and vanished.

"That thing just about scared me out of my skin!" Jillian said.

"I've had enough scares for one day," Katrina said. "I want to go home."

"We all do," I said. "But right now, it's too dangerous to try to make it through the woods. I think the safest place will be on the other side of the fence."

"I hope that deer doesn't get eaten," Jillian said.

"Hopefully," I said, "the deer will be faster than those lizards. She'll probably be able to outrun them."

We kept walking until we came to the tear in the fence. I pulled the two sides apart, and Jillian slipped through, followed by Katrina, then me. This time, I didn't get my shirt caught on any of the sharp wires.

"I didn't even know this place was here," Katrina said.

"We didn't either," I replied as I shook my head. "I don't know what it is, but I don't think anyone is around."

We walked to the building. Once again, I knocked on the door, just in case someone was inside and hadn't heard me the first time. There was no answer, and I stepped away from the door.

And that's when we heard something. It was just a light shuffling, and I really couldn't tell what the noise was. But it was definitely a sound, and it definitely came from inside the odd, cone-shaped building.

"Someone is inside!" Jillian said.

I knocked on the door again. "Is someone there?" I called out. "Please . . . we need help. Is anyone there?"

I waited, but no one came to the door.

"I know I heard something," I said.

"We did, too," Katrina said. "Knock again."

I banged my fist on the door. "Please," I said. "If anyone is inside, please help us."

Still, no one came to the door.

Katrina strode to a nearby window and peered inside.

"These windows are like mirrors," she said. "But I think I can see inside." She leaned forward. Her face was only inches from the glass when she suddenly leapt back, screaming at the top of her lungs!

Katrina jumped so suddenly that she tripped and fell to the ground. Immediately, she leapt to her feet and pointed at the window.

"There's a monster in there!" she shrieked. "One of those . . . those *things* is in there!"

"What?!?!" I said. "A Komodo dragon?"

Katrina nodded, still pointing at the window. "One of them is in there!" she exclaimed. "I saw him! He saw me!"

I walked to where Katrina was standing and looked where she was pointing.

"But the glass is mirrored," I said. "How did you see

something?"

"If you get up close," Katrina replied, "you can see through. Not very well, but I know what I saw. And I saw one of those things looking back at me!"

I was wary, but I decided to see for myself. Katrina has a habit of imagining things, and this was probably one of those times. I doubted there was actually a Komodo dragon inside the building.

But, I thought, *maybe she's right. After all: Komodo dragons shouldn't even be in Kentucky. It's possible Katrina is right.*

Cautiously, I took a step toward the window. Then another, and another. Finally, I was only a few inches from the glass. Katrina was right: being close to the glass made a difference. I could see my reflection in the mirror-like material, but I could also see dark shapes and forms on the other side.

Other than that, however, I saw nothing. Oh, I could see what appeared to be a table with a few odds and ends on it. But nothing that looked like a Komodo dragon.

"Do you see him?" Katrina asked.

I shook my head. "No," I replied.

"You don't believe me, do you?" Katrina said.

"I'm sure you saw something," I replied.

"Well, maybe he moved," Katrina said, "but I know

what I saw. It was one of those things—one of those Komodo dragons that tried to chew me up."

"Let's look in some of the other windows," Jillian suggested.

"Let me try the door one more time," I said. I walked to the door and pounded hard with my fist. I was sure if there was someone inside, they would have heard the knocking.

I waited, but no one came. I stepped to the right and walked to the closest window. Leaning close, I peered inside. I saw what appeared to be a room, but it was empty.

I went to the next window, and the next. Mostly, there wasn't anything to see. When I'd worked my way around the entire building, I met up with Katrina and Jillian at the front.

"Nothing," I said. "It's hard to see in the windows, anyway. But I didn't see anything."

Suddenly, we heard another noise from inside the building. This time, however, it seemed closer to the door.

"There is someone inside!" Jillian said.

I hustled to the door and knocked. "Hello?" I said loudly. "Is someone there? We really need help."

There was a scuffling sound on the other side of the door. Suddenly, there was a scrape and a whooshing noise, and the door slid open like an elevator panel.

Now, I had expected a man or a woman—certainly a human—to open the door. But I never expected to see the strange creature that was now staring back at me.

21

It wasn't a Komodo dragon . . . it was worse. Oh, it was a lizard of some sort, but he looked like he was half-human and half-lizard. The thing stood on two legs, and his skin was rough and leathery, like a lizard. But his arms, legs, and head were oddly human-like, and he had no tail like a lizard. He stood tall, about the size of an average man. It was the most bizarre creature I had ever seen in my life.

Two feelings hit me at the same time. First of all, I was terrified. The thing I was looking at was the scariest thing I'd ever seen.

But secondly, I was also filled with a strange sense of curiosity. Something inside of me wondered if what I was seeing was actually real. Could I actually be having some sort of strange dream? Would I awake in a moment and realize everything that had happened only in my mind while I was sleeping?

Then, Katrina and Jillian were both screaming. They began to run, and I figured that was the best thing to do, too. I spun and raced after them as they headed for the hole in the fence. Jillian reached it first, and she dove through. Katrina followed, and I was right behind her.

But before I went through the fence, I snapped around.

The lizard-man was coming after us!

He was running on his hind legs, like a human, but he was a bit slower and cumbersome. I wasn't sure how fast he could run . . . and I didn't want to find out.

"Hurry, Jason!" Jillian shrieked. *"He's coming!"*

I dove through the hole in the fence, tumbled to the ground, and got up. The three of us started to follow the driveway, in a last-ditch effort to save ourselves. Sure, there was the threat of the Komodo dragons, as they could be lurking anywhere in the forest.

But at the moment, we had another problem to worry about: the strange thing that had emerged from the building and was now chasing us. I was sure he was just as dangerous as the giant, vicious Komodo dragons.

Our shoes smacking the hard packed ground was the only sound we heard. The three of us tore down the driveway, not looking back . . . until I felt a claw on my shoulder. I tried to wiggle free, to pull away, but it was no use. The creature pulled hard, knocking me off balance and sending me sprawling to the ground. Then, everything went black.

22

I wasn't knocked unconscious or anything, but I'd closed my eyes before I hit the ground, knowing it was all over for me. The last thing I thought as I hit the ground was a tiny hope that Jillian and Katrina would be able to get away. For me, it was too late.

I felt the weight of the creature upon me, pinning me to the ground. I could feel his claws on my neck and shoulders, and I knew the next thing I felt was going to be sharp teeth and claws plunging into my skin, tearing me to shreds. I could only hope my end would come quickly.

But I felt no pain. In fact, the claws released their grip on me. Suddenly, the weight was off me, and I was free.

I rolled over. The creature was standing over me, looking at me curiously. Although he looked just as hideous as ever, it didn't seem like he was going to hurt me. Still, I began to crawl away and was about to take off running, when he spoke.

"Don't be afraid," he said. His voice was very strange: deep and gravelly. He sounded hoarse, like it was an effort for him to speak.

"You . . . you can talk?" I managed to ask.

"Not very well," the creature said. "It is difficult for me to communicate the way you do. But I am learning."

Now I was sure I was dreaming. I was dreaming, and I knew that, at any moment, I would wake up. Creatures like the one before me just didn't exist . . . except, of course, in dreams and nightmares.

I suddenly remembered Jillian and Katrina, and I looked around, but I didn't see them. They must have continued running to get away.

"What . . . what are you?" I asked.

"I'm not sure I can explain everything to you right now," the creature replied. "You would not understand. But it is not safe for you here. I can tell you more, but we must return to the laboratory, where it's safe."

"Laboratory?" I asked. "That's what that building

is?"

The creature nodded. "Yes. But we mustn't waste time. Let's go back, and I will explain everything to you."

"But my sister and her friend," I said, pointing down the driveway. "I have to find them."

At that very moment, Jillian and Katrina appeared. They were racing toward us.

"It's one of them!" Katrina shrieked. "He's after us!"

At first, I didn't know what she was talking about. Then, it became clear: coming after them was not one, but two giant Komodo dragons!

#

Seeing the enormous lizards chasing Jillian and Katrina was a shock. The creatures were so big they didn't look real. Like they were beasts from a video game that had leapt from the screen and into reality.

"We must hurry back to the laboratory," the creature said. "The dragons will not go through the fence."

Jillian and Katrina were still running toward us.

"We're doomed!" Katrina shouted. *"This time, we're really, really doomed!"*

"You can outrun them!" I urged. "Come on! Follow us!"

The strange lizard-man turned and ran. I leapt to my

feet and followed. Behind us, Jillian and Katrina were gaining, and the good news was they were leaving the Komodo dragons behind. Oh, the giant reptiles were still coming after them . . . but Jillian and Katrina kept running. They would be able to get away.

Ahead of me, I was shocked to see the lizard creature leap over the fence in a single bound! It was effortless for him. I wished I could have jumped the fence that easily, but I knew there was no way. Instead, I raced to the tear in the fence, stretched the mesh wires wide, and slipped through. I held the hole open for Jillian and Katrina, who were right behind me. They, too, scrambled through the hole in the fence. Katrina's arm caught one of the sharp edges of the fence, but luckily, it caused only a scratch.

We were safe . . . and on the other side of the fence, the Komodo dragons weren't at all happy about it. They snorted and clawed at the ground in anger, swishing their tails and lashing out with their tongues.

"They won't come any closer," the lizard-man said.

Jillian and Katrina stared in amazement at him. They were just as shocked as I had been when I first heard him speak.

"He's okay," I said. "He's not going to hurt us."

"How do you know?" Katrina asked. "You just met him. Maybe he brought us here so he could fry us like hamburgers and have us for lunch!"

"I have no intention of harming anyone," the creature said in that rough, raspy voice. "I'm sorry you are even here."

"But," I began, "what is 'here?' What is this place?"

"It might be better if I explain and show you a few things at the same time," the creature replied.

"Do you have a name?" I asked.

"Yes," the creature said with a nod. "But you are not able to pronounce it in your language, so you may call me whatever you wish."

"How about 'Freakazoid?'" Katrina said.

I turned and glared at her. *"Knock it off!"* I hissed under my breath.

"Sorry," she peeped. "But it seems fitting."

"How about we call you something simple," I said. "Like Karl?"

"Karl," the creature said in his deep, raspy voice. "Yes, Karl does sound good. You may call me Karl."

My mind suddenly drifted back over the things that had occurred since morning, which now seemed like years ago. I remembered Jillian taking her time trying to find the right shirt. I remembered hiking in the woods and finding the lizard in the tree, and Katrina grabbing my ankle. I remembered using Mom's computer to discover that what we'd seen was a baby Komodo dragon, then finding the giant lizards and being attacked. And I remembered thinking Katrina had been eaten, only to discover she was unhurt. So many crazy things had happened that morning that I knew no one would believe me if I told them. Nothing seemed to make sense . . . yet.

But it was about to.

Karl was about to explain what was really going on . . . and that was more unbelievable than anything else I'd ever experienced in my entire life . . . .

The door to Karl's laboratory was wide open, and Karl gestured to it. "Come inside," he said.

"This sure is a funny-shaped laboratory," Katrina said as she stared at the building.

I was a little hesitant to go inside, but something told me everything was going to be okay. After all: I didn't have any idea about what was going on, but I was sure Karl wasn't going to hurt us.

On the other hand, the giant creatures on the other side of the fence seemed as threatening as ever, and I knew that, if they had the chance, they would tear us apart. It was a frightening thought, and I was glad we were safe.

"Why won't the lizards go near the fence?" I asked as we made our way to the laboratory.

"They used to," Karl said. "I thought the fence would stop them, but it didn't. One of them tore a hole in it and came through. So, I attached an electric wire to the fence. Being made of metal, the fence conducted the electricity all around. That worked . . . for a short time. Yesterday, it quit working, and I don't know why. But the 'lizards' as you call them still believe the fence is electrified, so they stay away from it."

"You mean that if we had been here yesterday and touched the fence, we would have been electrocuted?" Jillian asked.

"Yes, that is correct," Karl said in his deep, raspy voice.

"I'm shocked," Katrina said, and I looked back at her and rolled my eyes.

"Wait a minute," Jillian said as we entered the building. "Where did you get the fence? I mean . . . looking the way you do, you can't just go into a hardware store and buy material."

"You're getting ahead of things," Karl said as we entered a large room. It was filled with all sorts of mechanical and electrical gadgets. In fact, it looked more like some sort of control room. There were computer monitors on the walls and hundreds of buttons, switches, and dials. It would probably take somebody years to figure out how to use all of them.

"What's all this stuff for?" I asked as my eyes swept the room.

Karl raised his hands, and for the first time, I got a good look at them. They were similar to human hands, except, of course, they looked like rough leather. His fingers were longer than a human's, and his fingernails were longer, too, resembling the claws of the Komodo dragons, although they didn't appear to be as sharp.

"One thing at a time," he said. "I can explain, but I don't think you'll understand all I have to tell you. It is far more complicated than you know."

"I'm already confused," Jillian said.

"Well," Karl said, "the truth is that—"

A noise in another room interrupted Karl, and he stopped speaking. Then, without warning, a huge Komodo dragon appeared in the hall!

25

Katrina shrieked. Jillian's hands flew to her mouth, stifling her scream. I don't know if I screamed or gasped or whatever . . . but I sure was freaked out!

Karl was quick to speak. "Don't worry," he said. "Perhaps this will be a good place to begin. Watch."

The enormous Komodo dragon filled the hallway. He plodded slowly toward us, and his claws scratched the floor, making thick scraping sounds. Karl spoke to the creature in some weird language that sounded like gibberish; it certainly wasn't anything close to English or any other normal language.

The Komodo dragon stopped moving, but only for

a moment. Then, he began to move very slowly . . . but he didn't move forward or backward. Instead, his body began to twist, like he was doing some kind of weird stretching exercises. Soon, his bones began to shift all around, and his entire shape began to change. His front feet rose from the floor, and his fingers and claws became shorter. His tail retracted into his body. We could see bones beneath his thick skin, moving, shifting, and twisting.

I watched with wide eyes and my mouth open in total disbelief. The Komodo dragon was no longer a lizard . . . he had changed completely! He had turned into the same kind of creature as Karl! His leathery skin was creamy beige with a few dark brown patches, and his eyes were black, liquid orbs.

Behind me, I heard my sister gasp. I took a step back and stood next to her and Katrina, but I couldn't stop staring at the creature in the hallway. I remember reading a book once, about a girl in Saginaw, Michigan, who could change herself into a spider. I thought that was freaky . . . but this was far more bizarre than that!

"We are not what you think we are," Karl said. "I believe you would refer to us as 'reptiles,' but that is not what we are at all."

Jillian, Katrina, and I continued staring. None of us spoke.

"You see," Karl continued, "the truth is that the lizards you have seen in the woods—Komodo dragons, you call them—are not even creatures from this planet. They—and this includes myself—are from a planet millions of miles from here."

"You're . . . you're space aliens?" Jillian stammered.

"If that is what you call someone from another planet," Karl replied, "then, yes, that is what we are." He pointed at the creature in the hall. "This is my brother. We are here to solve a problem."

"What problem?" I asked.

"Last year," Karl said, "one of our spaceships crashed here. The craft was destroyed, but our kind survived. The problem they faced was that in order to survive on your planet, they needed to adapt."

"What's that mean?" Jillian asked.

"It means they had to change to survive," Karl answered. "They learned to turn into creatures that walk on all fours, so they could better hunt for food. They grew tails to use as powerful weapons and longer claws and teeth. But the problem was, after living on your planet, they forgot that they were actually not of this Earth. They forgot where they came from. With no way to return to our planet, they had no choice but to remain here, on Earth. They have no idea of their true nature and do not know that they are actually from another planet, millions of miles away."

"They forgot that they're space aliens?" Katrina asked.

Karl nodded, and his brother spoke. "The only reason they have attacked you is they feel threatened. Otherwise, they would leave you alone. Like us, they have no intention of hurting anyone. But they have lost their identity and don't know what they really are. My brother and I came here in hopes of gathering our kind and returning to our planet." He looked at Karl. "And I think we're going to succeed. The computer chip, I believe, will work."

"That is great news," Karl replied.

I really couldn't believe what I was hearing. I couldn't believe what I was seeing, either, but there they were, right in front of me: two aliens from outer space. I mean . . . it was strange enough to see giant Komodo dragons in the forest, but it was even weirder to think they weren't really lizards at all!

"How many of them—of you—are there?"

"Six adults and six little ones," Karl replied.

"And you have to catch them?" Katrina asked.

Karl's brother shook his head. "Not catch them," he said. "We must implant each one of them with a special computer microchip that will send a signal to their brain, causing them to fall into a deep sleep. While they are sleeping, the microchip will reprogram their intellectual senses, and when they wake, they will change back into their normal selves. Then, we'll all be able to go home."

"Speaking of going home," I said, "it's getting late. We've got to be getting back to our home, too." While I was really fascinated with Karl and his brother, I felt like we were getting in a bit over our heads, and the best thing to do was go home where we knew we'd be safe.

"We'll take you through the forest," Karl's brother said. "It's too dangerous to go out on your own."

"But what will we do if one of those things comes after us?" I asked. "Or two of them?"

"We'll be ready," Karl's brother said. "As long as you're with us, there's nothing to worry about."

Well, as it turns out, we were about to discover we had a lot to worry about.

26

Karl's brother turned, walked down the hall, and vanished into another room. He returned with a black object about the size of a small baseball bat. It had the characteristics of a gun, with a short handle and a trigger.

"This is what we'll use to implant the computer chip under their skin," Karl's brother said.

"You have to shoot them with it?" I asked.

Karl shook his head. "No," he replied. "The computer microchips are loaded inside, but the device must actually touch the skin."

"But how are you going to get close enough to them?" Jillian asked.

"Simple," Karl's brother replied. "I'll just change back into a lizard shape. They won't even know the difference, and they'll think I'm one of them. It will be harder to carry the microchip injector with longer claws, but I'll have to make it work."

"What if something goes wrong?" Jillian asked. "What if one of them wants to fight you?"

"By then, I'll be close enough to implant the chip," Karl's brother said. "Instantly, it will send a message to their brain, putting them into a deep sleep. Meanwhile, the computer microchip will reprogram their brain. When they awake, they'll realize the true nature of their identity and change back into their original selves."

"I hope it works," I said, "but we really need to get going. If we're late, our mom is going to be really mad."

"Yeah," said Katrina, "and if we get eaten by giant lizards, they're going to be even madder."

"We will help you return," Karl said, "but I must ask you this: tell no one what you have seen today. We are here only for a short time. Your people and your world are not ready for the knowledge of us."

"I'm not sure if I'm ready," Katrina said.

We walked outside and into the bright sunshine. I was really glad we would finally be on our way home, and I felt safer with Karl and his brother with us. They were bigger and stronger than we were, and I knew if any of those creatures came along, we'd be safe.

Boy, was I in for a surprise.

27

We followed Karl and his brother as they walked to the gate. I found it strange that I thought of Karl's brother only as 'his brother,' and I wondered if we should make up a name for him.

Probably not, I thought. After all: we probably won't get a chance to know him very well. We'll be home soon, and if Karl and his brother are successful, they won't be around for very long.

The whole thing seemed very bizarre. Lots of people believe in space aliens from other planets even though they've never seen them, and Jillian, Katrina, and I were probably the only people in the world who had actually come into contact—face-to-face—with beings from another galaxy!

We strode to the gate where Karl grasped the combination lock in his claws and dialed in the code. The lock clicked open, and the chain fell away. He pushed the gate, it swung wide, and we walked through. Then, he closed the gate behind him.

"We won't need to lock it anymore," Karl said.

We walked in a tight knot, the five of us, until we reached the edge of the forest. Then, we stopped.

"Do you know which direction your house is?" Karl asked.

"Well," I said, pointing. "The sun is over there, so that would probably mean that our house is over that way." I pointed in the opposite direction. "We'll at least be able to find our neighborhood. We were a little lost earlier, but I'm pretty sure that if we go that way, we'll at least be going in the right direction."

"Let's all stay close," Karl's brother said. "Be watchful."

We started out into the forest. I tried to be quiet, but so many branches and small trees made it impossible. We sounded like a herd of elk wandering through a bag of potato chips.

But we weren't the only ones making a commotion,

and it wasn't long before we heard a noise in the distance. Karl heard it first, and he stopped walking and raised his claw, urging us to stop. The five of us stood motionless, listening.

Not far away, we could hear the crackling sounds of branches and brush being moved and trampled.

"Is it one of those things?" Katrina whispered.

"I can't see anything yet," I whispered back.

We listened, and suddenly, we heard another sound. *Voices.*

I relaxed. It wasn't one of those creatures, after all. It sounded like people—two boys, in fact—and they were getting closer by the moment.

"You and I must hide," Karl's brother said to Karl. "It will be dangerous for us if we are discovered by anyone else."

"We'll stay right here," I said. "If they get close, we'll try to steer them in another direction."

Not far away was a thick stand of small trees. Karl and his brother hustled over to them, ducked down, and became invisible. Of course, they didn't vanish, but they blended in with the leaves and branches so well it was difficult to see them.

Meanwhile, we could hear the boys getting closer. They were being noisy and loud, talking and laughing.

"There they are," Jillian said, pointing.

Two boys, a couple of years older than us, appeared. Each was wearing blue jeans; one had a white T-shirt, the other was wearing a black tank top. They both had dark brown hair. One of them was carrying something that looked like a rolled-up towel. They saw us at the same time we saw them and stopped talking. They looked at us curiously as they approached.

"Hey," the one in the white shirt said, "you kids seen any lizards around here?"

I looked at Jillian, and she looked at me.

"No," I said. I knew it wasn't the truth, but something told me the kids were up to no good.

"I saw a lizard in a tree this morning," the boy continued. "He was as long as my arm. I'm going to catch him and keep him as a pet."

"That might not be a good idea," I said. "What if he bites you?"

"He isn't going to bite me," the boy said. "I'm too fast. I'm going to catch him in my net and take him home."

I almost laughed. After all: he had the same idea I'd had . . . until I found out what the Komodo dragons actually were.

But the two boys had no idea what kind of danger they were in. How were they supposed to know that what they'd seen wasn't a lizard, but a space alien? How were they to know that some of them were enormous and could swallow them in a single gulp?

"I don't think it's a good idea," I said again. "You might get hurt."

The kid in the black tank top glared at me. "You've got to be kidding," he said. "Come on, Tony. These kids are just chicken. Let's go find that lizard."

They turned and started walking away through the forest. Thankfully, they didn't see Karl and his brother hiding in the brush. They would have been in for a shock, for sure!

When they were gone, Karl and his brother emerged from their hiding place.

"It's dangerous for them to be here," Karl said in his low, gravelly voice.

And he was right. At that very instant, we heard one of the boys screaming in terror!

28

The five of us sprang, charging through the forest, heading in the direction of the screams. Of course, the two boys would now see Karl and his brother, but if they had encountered one of those giant lizard aliens, they were going to need help. Maybe Karl's brother could get close enough to implant a computer microchip.

We came to a small clearing and saw the two boys . . . but no Komodo dragon. Karl and his brother ducked quickly out of sight—at least for the time being. They didn't want to be seen if they didn't have to.

We ran up to the boys. Both of them were cowering back from something on the ground, in the grass.

A baby Komodo dragon? I wondered. What could possibly be scaring them so much?

"What is it?" Katrina asked as we approached the boys.

The one wearing the black tank top pointed at the ground. "A snake!" he screeched. "I hate snakes!"

I looked where he was pointing and nearly burst out laughing. I expected to see a large rattlesnake, coiled and threatening . . . but it was only a harmless garter snake! Not only that, it wasn't even a very big garter snake.

"That snake isn't going to hurt you," I said. "He's just a garter snake."

"I don't care!" the kid said. "Snakes freak me out!"

The snake began to wiggle away, causing the boys to shriek even more.

"Sheesh," Jillian whispered. "I can't believe they're that freaked out by a harmless garter snake."

The two boys whirled and ran off, still shrieking.

"Well," Katrina said, "at least we won't have to worry about them."

"I just hope they make it home safe," I said.

"I hope we make it home safe," said Jillian.

"Karl!" I called out. "It's okay! They were scared off by a garter snake!"

We waited for them to come out of hiding, but they

didn't.

"Karl?" I called out. "Where are you?"

"They went over that way," Katrina said, pointing. We looked, but we didn't see them.

"Karl?" I called out again.

"Looks like they split," Katrina said. "I've always said you can never count on space aliens."

I looked at her and rolled my eyes. Katrina was always trying to be funny like that.

"Well, let's keep going on our own," I said. "I'm pretty sure we need to go that way." I pointed. "In fact, I don't think we're too far from home."

We headed out again, and all I could think about were the things that had happened to us today. Would anyone believe us? Our story seemed so farfetched that I didn't think anyone would take us seriously. Even Mom. When you start talking about lizards that are actually space aliens from another planet, people probably look at you funny. And they'd never believe you, for sure.

"Hey!" Katrina said. "Look! There's a trail, up ahead!"

She was right! We'd come upon one of the main trails that wound through the forest. I recognized it right away, and I knew exactly where we were. Most important, I knew exactly where we needed to go.

"We'll be home in five minutes!" Jillian exclaimed.

And we would have been, too . . . if it wasn't for something that was waiting for us behind a large, old tree.

29

When I heard the rustling of leaves and the snapping of branches, I didn't think it was a Komodo dragon. In fact, I was sure it wasn't. I was sure it was Karl or his brother, or both of them. Maybe it was the two older boys.

But I was wrong.

A large lizard head suddenly rose up. His mouth was open, and I couldn't believe the size of his teeth! They were gigantic. With teeth like that, he could tear the three of us to shreds in no time at all . . . and I was sure he was going to try.

"Climb a tree!" I screeched. *"It's our only chance!"*

Thankfully, luck was on our side. There were a

number of trees close by, and most of them had large, low branches, making them perfect for climbing. Each of us ran to separate trees, grabbed the first branch, and pulled ourselves up . . . and just in time, too. The giant Komodo dragon was lunging toward us, but he was confused for a moment, not sure which one of us to go after. It was an extra split second we needed, and the three of us were able to scramble high enough so the alien Komodo dragon couldn't reach us. He charged angrily from tree trunk to tree trunk and tried to climb with his front legs, but he wasn't strong enough to pull himself up. I found a sturdy branch and held on, watching the creature below.

"This is getting really, really old!" Katrina said. "I'm been almost doomed more times today than I ever have!"

"But you're alive!" I shouted. "And we're almost home!"

"We can't go home while that thing is hanging around," Jillian said. She, too, had stopped climbing. She had her arms wrapped around two branches, and she was watching the Komodo dragon below.

"Now what?" Katrina hollered.

"We wait," I said. "Sooner or later, that thing will go away. Or Karl and his brother will show up. If we just hang out, we'll be all right."

"Oh, I get it," Katrina shouted back. "Hang out.

Funny."

Below me, the Komodo dragon was sniffing around the trunk of the tree. I again noticed his size, and I couldn't help but think about how crazy this day had become.

Komodo dragons that are actually aliens from outer space, I thought. How freaky is that?

I was watching the creature as he made his way around the tree, thankful I was safely off the ground. So, you can imagine my surprise when I heard a sudden crack!, and the branch I was clinging to snapped. I tried to grab another one and hold on, but it was too late. I was already falling . . . straight down into the gaping mouth of the waiting Komodo dragon!

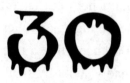

I flailed my arms in a desperate attempt to grasp anything, but there was nothing to grab hold of. I screamed as I fell . . . and landed squarely on the back of the creature!

He made a deep grunting sound when I landed. I think I surprised him, as I don't think he was prepared for his next meal to fall out of the tree.

But I was alive . . . at least for the moment. I was on his back, and I quickly wrapped my arms around his neck. He turned his head and tried to snap at me, but he couldn't reach me. He opened his mouth, snorted, and again tried to bite at me, but he couldn't get his head turned around far enough. Which, of course, was lucky for me.

"Hang on, Jason!" my sister screamed. *"Hang on tight!"*

Of course, she didn't have to tell me that. There was no way I was going to let go. Sure, it was probably the last place in the world I wanted to be, but if I let go, that thing would have me for dinner.

And I couldn't help but have the feeling I was a contestant in some strange, interplanetary rodeo. I had become the rookie bronco rider, a true space cadet, and I was being tossed madly about by an angry, alien Komodo dragon. Trouble was, if he threw me off, he wouldn't just trot away like a horse in a corral. He'd rear back, attack, and wolf me down like a cupcake in two seconds flat. The only thing I could do was hang on and hope for—

For what?

Sooner or later, my strength would wear down. I couldn't hold on forever. The creature was obviously much stronger than I was. And it didn't seem like there was much chance Karl and his brother coming to the rescue.

In an effort to throw me off, the alien lizard made a sharp, violent twist to the right, then a quick turn back to the left. My hold around his neck slipped a little, but I managed to hang on. But my head snapped around wildly, and I caught a flashbulb glimpse of tree branches.

That gave me an idea. It was crazy, of course, but it

was the only chance I might have.

If he gets close to a tree with a low branch, I thought, I might be able to grab it and pull myself up.

Sure, it was a long shot. But I really didn't have any other options, and I didn't know how long I'd be able to hang on around the creature's neck before he threw me off.

Then, of course, it would be all over. If that happened, I'd never be fast enough to get away.

The creature bounded close to a tree, and I saw a branch I could grab . . . if only I was closer. However, there wasn't anything I could do to control the raging creature. It wasn't like I could grab some reins and steer him in any direction I wanted. Right now, he was going to go anywhere he wanted.

And man, was he full of energy! He bucked and twisted and snapped around, constantly trying to get me off his back. But I held fast. It seemed to me the longer I held on, the madder the alien Komodo dragon became.

Suddenly, luck was on my side. He made a quick spin to the right, and the tree branch was right above my head. Without thinking for a moment longer, I let go of the Komodo dragon's neck, reached up, and pulled with all my might. I swung my legs up and looped them over the branch. Then, I grabbed for a higher branch and struggled to pull myself up farther.

"Look out, Jason!" Jillian shrieked. "He's trying to get you!"

I didn't dare take the time to look. Instead, I concentrated on pulling myself up, higher and higher, where I would be safe. I kept waiting for the beast to strike, to feel his enormous teeth sink into my flesh, but the assault never came. Once again, I had been lucky. My heart was galloping like a racehorse, and I was out of breath, but I was alive.

Then, and only then, did I take a moment to look down. Beneath me, circling the tree trunk, was the alien Komodo dragon. He was looking up at me with sinister, angry eyes, furious I had escaped.

I turned my head up, looking for Jillian and Katrina, but I didn't see them. There were too many branches and leaves.

"I'm okay!" I called out to them, just to let them know I hadn't been eaten.

"You got lucky!" Katrina exclaimed. "I thought you were doomed!"

Well, I wasn't doomed, after all. I was safe in the tree. But for someone else, things were about to take a turn for the worse. Because just then, I heard voices.

Two boys.

The same kids that said they were going to try to catch one of the baby Komodo dragons. I could hear them laughing and joking, and their voices were getting louder.

They were coming closer.

Beneath me, the Komodo dragon stopped circling. He, too, had heard the boys coming.

I had been lucky; I had been able to escape.

The two boys, however, weren't going to be so fortunate.

In Katrina's words: they were doomed.

31

Although I couldn't see them yet, I shouted out a warning to the two boys.

"Hey, you guys!" I yelled. "Don't come any closer! Run away, quick!"

The boys stopped talking to one another.

"Where are you?" one of the boys called out.

"I'm in a tree!" I shouted back. "I was attacked by a—"

I almost said 'alien Komodo dragon,' but I caught myself. They'd think I was crazy if I told them that!

"—a giant lizard!" I said. "And he's about to attack you!"

I could hear the boys speaking to one another, but I couldn't make out what they were saying. Meanwhile, the alien Komodo dragon beneath me had assumed an assault position. He was crouched low with his head down in concentration. His tongue feathered out of his mouth, back and forth, back and forth.

"Where is he?" one of the boys called out. "We want to catch him."

"Not this one, you don't!" I shouted. "Go home now, or you'll be sorry!"

"You just don't want us to catch him!" one of the boys shouted back.

"I don't want you to get eaten!" I shouted. "Now, go home, or you'll be sorry!"

Below me, the Komodo dragon slowly began to move, crawling stealthily forward, his head down and eyes focused. As he continued to move away from the tree, I began climbing down slowly. I wasn't going to put myself in danger, but I wanted to get a better view of where the two boys were and try to convince them of the danger they were in.

"Something's moving over there!" I heard one of the boys shout. "Get the net ready!"

"You don't know what you're doing!" I yelled.

"That thing is bigger than both of you put together!"

"Listen to my brother!" Jillian shouted.

"If you guys know so much," one of the boys said, "then why don't you come out of hiding?"

"Yeah," the other kid called out. "Come down out of the trees."

"Why do you think we're hiding in trees?" Katrina snapped. "Both of you are doomed!"

The alien Komodo dragon was still stalking away, heading for the two boys. I climbed down to the last branch. Through the forest, I could see the two boys. From where they stood, they could see me, but the giant lizard was crouched low, and I knew the boys couldn't see him.

"There you are!" the kid in the black tank top said, pointing up at me.

"That lizard is coming for you," I warned.

"I know," the kid in the white T-shirt said. "I can see the branches moving. We're going to catch him."

He unrolled the net he'd been carrying. It wasn't very big, and there was no way he'd be able to use it to catch anything larger than a squirrel.

Suddenly, the alien Komodo dragon stopped moving. Incredibly, the two boys began walking toward it! They still couldn't see the creature, as it was laying low in the brush . . . but when they did, they were going to be in for

155

a surprise.

A movement from the left caught my attention. I turned and saw a disturbance in the woods: low branches and leaves shuddering.

Is it another one? I wondered.

"He's around here, somewhere," the kid in the white T-shirt said. Both boys were still slowly making their way to the alien Komodo dragon, which was flat on his belly, waiting to strike.

Then, just when I thought things couldn't get any worse, they did.

The disturbance in the woods to my left was, indeed, another giant Komodo dragon. It charged with lightning speed, and there was no way the two boys would have any chance to escape.

32

The sudden movement caught the attention of the two boys, along with the alien Komodo dragon that had been stalking them. When the two kids saw the monstrous beast charging them, they screamed.

"RUN!" I shouted, but I knew it was no use. The two boys were going to be lizard food. There was no way they could escape two charging Komodo dragons.

However, I was surprised to find the alien Komodo dragon attacking from my left wasn't after the two boys . . . he was charging the other lizard! In seconds, the two beasts were at each other, a mass of leather and muscle, lashing claws and gnashing teeth. They growled and snapped with the ferocity of fighting lions.

Horrified, the two boys ran in the other direction, yelping like scared dogs as they vanished into the woods. Maybe they hadn't been very smart, but they had been lucky, and that alone probably saved their lives.

And not far away, the two alien Komodo dragons were really going at each other. But as I watched, I noticed something strange. One of the creatures seemed like he was being cautious, like he didn't want to hurt the other one. He stepped aside when the other one lunged, and he didn't seem as fierce.

Then, out of nowhere, Karl appeared. He burst from the forest, carrying the implant gun, racing toward the two fighting beasts.

Suddenly, one of the creatures drew back. The other one looked puzzled and was about to lunge again when Karl reached him. He pressed the implant gun to its back. There was a soft pop! sound, and the giant lizard spun around angrily, ready to strike.

But it didn't have a chance. In the next instant, the creature's legs gave way, and the giant beast fell to the ground, motionless.

Instantly, the other alien Komodo dragon began to squirm and wiggle, and I realized what was happening.

It was Karl's brother! He had turned into a Komodo

dragon to distract the other alien creature! Not only had he saved the lives of the two boys, but he'd been able to distract the giant lizard long enough for Karl to use the implant gun and insert the microchip under its skin, causing it to fall asleep!

"Karl!" I exclaimed. "Man, you showed up at just the right time!"

"This is the last one," he said. "We were able to locate the others and implant the computer microchips. Now, we can all return to our planet."

Jillian and Katrina began climbing down from their perches high in the trees.

"I thought you were doomed for sure," Katrina hollered down.

"You think everything is doomed," I replied, shaking my head. Then, I turned to Karl and pointed at the giant alien Komodo dragon slumbering on the ground. "What are you going to do with him?" I asked.

"We'll carry him back to the laboratory where we've taken the others," Karl replied.

"How are you going to—"

A faint, distant shout echoed through the forest. It was Mom, calling out to Jillian and me.

I cupped my hands around my mouth. "We're coming, Mom!" I shouted. Then, I turned to Karl. There were so many more things I wanted to know, but I'd never have the chance to ask him.

"We have to go," I said. "Will you be here tomorrow?"

Karl shook his head. "We will be returning to our planet as soon as possible," he said.

"Well," I replied. "Travel safe."

Nothing more was said. No good-byes, nothing. Jillian, Katrina, and I simply turned and began walking away. When I looked back, Karl and his brother had each picked up one end of the alien Komodo dragon and were carrying it away.

"That's the freakiest thing that's ever happened to me in my entire life," she said. "I don't think I've ever been doomed so many times in one day."

"We were lucky," Jillian said. "But the problem is: no one is going to believe us."

"Mom will," I said, although I wasn't so sure. When we started telling her about space aliens that can change into Komodo dragons, she might just think we'd flipped our lids.

Ahead of us, our house came into view through the trees.

"We made it," Jillian said with a sigh of relief.

And that's when the ground started shaking beneath our feet. We stopped walking and looked at one another.

"What's going on?!?!" Katrina asked. Her eyes were wide and filled with fear.

"I don't know," I said as I looked around frantically. Even the trees were shaking.

Then, we heard what sounded like a distant airplane. The three of us turned and looked up into the sky. All we could do was stare in disbelief.

33

Rising into the sky above the treetops was an object. Not a plane or a helicopter, though.

"That's . . . that's—" Katrina stammered.

"That's a spaceship!" I exclaimed. "That's the alien spacecraft!"

The ship looked like a rocket, with a long nose cone . . . and that's when I realized something else.

"That building in the field!" I shouted. "That wasn't a building at all! That was the top of their spaceship! It must have been buried in the ground! Karl and his brother and all the other aliens are heading back to their planet!"

We watched in awe as the spacecraft shot higher and

higher into the sky. There was no plume of smoke or flame behind it, and I wondered how it was powered. By now, the ground had stopped trembling, and the sound of the spacecraft was faint. Soon, it was only a speck in the sky. Then, it was gone.

"We actually set foot in an alien spaceship!" Jillian said. "I'll bet we're the only people in the world who have done that!"

"I can't wait to tell my parents!" Katrina said. "I'll see you guys later!" And with that, she took off running up the trail, through our backyard, and vanished around the side of the house.

Jillian and I raced to our house and flew through the back door. Mom was in her office. We started chattering like crazy monkeys until Mom raised her hand.

"Hang on, hang on," she said. "One at a time."

I quickly told her about the Komodo dragons and how they weren't reptiles at all. I told her about Karl and his brother and the spaceship. All the while, Mom looked at me, nodding. However, as she listened, she began to smile.

"You don't believe me, do you?" I asked.

Mom just smiled and shook her head.

"It really happened, Mom!" Jillian insisted. Her eyes were wide and her face glowed with excitement. "Didn't you hear the spacecraft take off a few minutes ago? Didn't

164

you feel the ground shake?"

Mom shook her head. "I think I heard an airplane close by," she said, "but I was on the phone, and I didn't pay any attention. And I didn't feel the house shake."

"That wasn't an airplane!" I insisted as I pointed up. "That was the alien spacecraft!"

No matter what we said, Mom wouldn't believe us. She thought it was a good story and that we should write it down for other people to read. Maybe so, but nobody would believe it really happened. They would think we made up the whole thing.

"My parents didn't believe me, either," Katrina said. She came over after dinner, and the three of us sat under a tree in our front yard, talking about what had happened during the day.

"I have an idea," I said. "Let's go back and find that field. There should be a big hole in the ground where the spaceship was. I'll take my camera, and we can get some pictures. Besides: I dropped my backpack, and maybe I can find it."

"Great idea," Katrina said. "It won't be dark for a while. Let's go."

I ran into the house and returned with my camera. "Ready," I said.

We walked around the house, through the back yard,

and began following the trail that wound through the forest. It was early evening, but it was still very warm. A few birds sang.

"Let's cut through the forest," I said, pointing. "The field is over that way."

"Let's not get lost again," Jillian said.

"Don't worry," I replied. "I know right where we're going."

And I did, too. I found my backpack, and we found the field without any trouble. The fence, of course, was still there. But there wasn't a big hole in the ground. Oh, the earth had been disturbed, that was for sure. But it was like a big hole had been dug and filled back in. Other than that, there wasn't much of anything to see. Still, I took some pictures.

"It doesn't look like a spaceship has been here," Katrina said.

"But we know the truth," I said. "Maybe no one will believe us, but we know what happened."

"This has been the strangest day," Jillian said. "I thought I was going to be doomed ten different times."

We left the field and headed through the forest, thinking that our crazy day was coming to an end, that our adventure was over.

Not quite.

166

While we were making our way back to the trail, Katrina suddenly stopped and pointed at something in the woods.

"Look at that!" she exclaimed. *"I can't believe it! I can't believe it!"*

34

From where I was standing, I couldn't see what Katrina was pointing at. I took a step toward her and tried to locate what she was pointing at.

Then, I saw it.

A gravestone!

It was dirty, gray and streaked with age, but there was no mistaking it.

"The old graveyard!" I exclaimed. "We found it! We finally found it!"

We skirted around small shrubs and trees, wading through tall grass, stepping over logs and stumps, until we reached the edge of the cemetery. Then, the three of us stopped . . . and stared.

"Wow," Jillian breathed. "It's here. It's really here."

For the next minute, no one spoke. Our gaze was fixed on the old cemetery, and our eyes drifted from headstone to headstone. All of them were very old, and the engraved letters had faded and softened. Most of them weren't even readable. Many small trees had grown up over the years, and tall grass grew, un-mowed for decades. A couple of the headstones had fallen over.

I couldn't believe our luck. We'd been looking for the old graveyard for a long time, and now we'd found it . . . and we weren't even trying to find it!

I whipped out my camera and took a few pictures. Mom would love to see them, and I decided I'd also print a few and take them to the historical museum, where they might even put them on display!

We remained silent as we strolled slowly through the old cemetery. It wasn't very big, and I counted only seventeen headstones. Still, it was very cool . . . and a little creepy. I wondered what it would be like after dark, with the moon high in the sky. If I was with my friends, it would be the perfect place to have a camp out and read scary stories with a flashlight.

"We'll have to remember how to get here," Katrina said, "so we can show all of our friends."

"Now I know why we had such a hard time finding it," Jillian said. "It's overgrown with so many small trees that it's nearly impossible to see."

"This has been the coolest day," I said. "A little crazy, but very cool. I wonder what else is going to happen before we get home?"

It was at that very moment I heard a soft ruffling sound. A movement to my left caught my eye, and I turned . . . only to see a ghost rising up from behind one of the headstones!

35

Jillian shrieked, and so did Katrina. They, too, were surprised by the ghost that was rising up in the graveyard.

Which, of course, wasn't a ghost at all.

It was a girl. A normal, average girl. A human. She was about my age, and she had very curly, blonde hair.

"Hey," she said. "Sorry about that. I didn't mean to scare you."

"You didn't scare me," Katrina said. "I just screamed because Jillian did."

"Why were you hiding behind the gravestone?" I asked.

"I didn't know who you guys were. Earlier, there

were two boys who chased me through the woods. I thought you were them."

"Was one of them wearing a white T-shirt?" I asked. The girl nodded. "Was the other one wearing a black tank top?"

Again, the girl nodded. "Do you know them?" she asked.

"Sort of," I replied. "They're troublemakers. But I don't think they're going to be coming back into the woods anytime soon."

"What are you doing out here?" Jillian asked.

"I just moved here from Connecticut," the girl replied. "Just last week. I was exploring the woods, and I found this old graveyard."

"We've been looking for this place for a long time," I said. "I'm surprised you found it."

"It's kind of creepy," Jillian said.

"Creepy?" the girl said. "You don't know what creepy is."

"What do you mean?" Katrina asked.

"I just had the creepiest thing happen to me," she replied. "At our old home in Connecticut."

I wondered how anything could be creepier than space aliens that could change into Komodo dragons, but I didn't say anything.

"What happened to you in Connecticut?" Jillian asked.

The girl frowned. "It's kind of hard to explain," she said, "because what happened was so strange. But if you want me to tell you, I will."

"Sure," I said. "But what happened to you?"

"It has to do with an old curse," the girl replied, "and coyotes."

A curse? I thought. Coyotes?

"Sounds freaky," Katrina said. "Were you doomed?"

Again, the girl nodded. "Doomed is a good word for it," she replied. Then, she began telling us her incredible story about the curse of the Connecticut coyotes . . . .

Next:

#28: Curse of the Connecticut Coyotes

Continue on for a FREE preview!

"Hey, Mom," I called out from my bedroom. "Have you seen my hairbrush?" I'd looked all over for it. Usually, it's on my dresser, but once in a while, I misplace it.

Like tonight.

"No, Erica, I haven't," Mom replied from the kitchen. "Did you check the bathroom?"

"Not yet," I said. Barefoot, I strode out of my bedroom, down the hall, into the bathroom, and turned on the light. I glanced around, but I didn't see any sign of my brush.

Where could it be? I wondered. I usually don't take it out of my bedroom.

Odd.

I turned off the light, left the bathroom, and walked to the kitchen where Mom was busy pulling out pots and pans.

"It's not in the bathroom, either," I said.

"I wouldn't know where it is," Mom replied. "Maybe gremlins stole it."

I rolled my eyes. Whenever something goes missing in our house, Mom blames it on gremlins. Usually it's Dad who loses things, and, usually, it's his car keys or his wallet. He gets really frustrated, and turns the house upside down in his attempt to find whatever it is that he's misplaced. And, of course, he usually finds the item in the exact place he put it.

Things are always found in the last place that you look, Mom always says.

Which makes a lot of sense. After all: once you find whatever it is you're looking for, you don't have to keep looking, because you've already found it . . . in the last place you look.

But I still had no clue where my hairbrush was, and I wanted to find it before I went to bed.

I stood in the kitchen, thinking, while Mom scurried about. She was experimenting with some kind of new cake recipe. Pots and pans were now stacked on the counter, and there were plastic bowls and utensils in the sink. She might be making a cake, but she was also making a mess. Mom is like that. She's a great cook, but she sure destroys the kitchen when she makes meals.

Through the kitchen window, a movement caught my attention. The sun was setting, and the sky was orange and purple. It would be dark soon.

But the motion that caught my attention was my little brother, Cole. He ran past the picnic table in the back yard and vanished out of sight. Cole is only three, and he's always getting into some sort of trouble, always making some kind of mischief. I'm eleven, so I'm a lot older . . . and I always seem to be bailing him out of trouble.

But he can be a pest, too.

Like now.

In the gloomy dusk, I saw something I recognized, sitting on the picnic table.

My hairbrush.

"There it is!" I said to Mom. "My brush is outside! What's it doing out there?"

"Maybe the gremlins left it there, Erica," Mom

replied without looking up from the mixing bowl in front of her.

Yeah, right, I thought. *Gremlins, nothing. Cole took my brush. He took my brush and left it out there.*

I stormed across the kitchen and slid open the glass door.

"Cole!" I shouted. "Where are you?!?!"

He didn't answer, but I could hear him at the far end of our back yard, where the grass ended and the trees began. With nightfall approaching, it was too dark to see him. But he was talking to himself, which is something else he does.

I strode across the grass to the picnic table. The blades were cold and wet against my bare feet. I could smell the thick scent of a wood fire, and I figured someone on the block was having a cookout. That's just what it's like in Fairfield, Connecticut. Lots of people have cookouts, barbecues, games, get-togethers . . . especially on our block. Everyone knows everyone, and we have a lot of fun. I have a lot of friends on our block, and we never run out of things to do.

I was just about to pick up my hairbrush from the picnic table when something Cole said caught my attention.

"Nice doggie," he said. "Pretty, pretty doggie."

I stopped and turned, straining to see in the gloom.

"Cole?" I called out. "Is there a dog with you?"

I was concerned. Cole was too young to know that it could be dangerous to pet unfamiliar dogs. He was too little to know that he should stay away from dogs running loose.

"Cole?" I said again, and I started walking toward his voice. "Is there a dog in the yard?"

As I drew closer, I could make out his white shirt, but it was still too dark to see anything else. He was just a ghostly form against a black curtain.

"Nice doggie," Cole said again. "Good doggie."

"Cole," I began, "You shouldn't—"

Suddenly, I saw the animal that Cole was speaking to, and I stopped speaking.

I froze.

My blood chilled.

Oh, no! I thought. *That's not a dog! That's MUCH worse!*

2

A skunk.

I could see the white strip on her back, and I could make out the shadowy form of her body. She wasn't very big, really—probably about the size of a normal cat—but that didn't matter. My little brother thought it was a dog!

"Cole," I said sternly, "come here *right now.*"

"I wanna play with the doggie," Cole said.

"Cole, that's not a dog," I said, drawing in a nervous breath. "That's a *skunk*. And if you don't come here this very minute, she's going to spray you and you're going to stink like a skunk."

"Huh-uh," Cole said. "I wanna play with the nice doggie."

I knew I had only seconds. It was only a matter of moments before the skunk would turn, raise her tail, and spray Cole. He'd stink for weeks! Not only that, he'd make our house stink. Everything in our home would smell like skunk . . . including *me*.

I decided to take a different approach. Instead of trying to order him to come to me, I decided to be nice.

"Cole," I said sweetly, "if you come to the house right now, I'll get you a big bowl of chocolate ice cream. I'll even put a scoop of peanut butter on it, just how you like."

Cole paused. Then: "Really?" he asked.

"Really," I replied. "But you have to come here, right now."

It worked. Cole turned and walked toward me. The skunk began waddling away.

I let out a sigh of relief. Cole had no idea how close he'd come to being sprayed. I've often called my brother a 'little stinker,' but I only meant it as a joke. If that skunk would have sprayed him, he would have been a *real* little stinker!

"I love ice cream!" Cole said.

"I know you do," I replied. I took him by the hand and we walked to the house together. "I'll hook you up with a big bowl, all for you."

"I can't find Teddy," Cole said.

"You lost your Teddy Bear?" I asked. Cole has a stuffed bear that he takes everywhere.

"Uh-huh," he replied.

"He'll turn up," I said. "Like Mom says: things are always found in the last place you look."

Inside our house, the mess in the kitchen had grown to monstrous proportions. There was flour and dough and cake mix all over the cupboards, the counter, and even on the floor. Mom was busy looking at a recipe, and she had a confused look on her face, like she was trying to figure something out. Like I said: Mom's a good cook, but when she makes something, she *destroys* the kitchen.

"Go get your pajamas on," I said to Cole, "and I'll get your ice cream."

"Goody!" Cole squealed, and he took off running to his bedroom. While he was gone, I explained to Mom about the skunk in the back yard, and how close Cole had come to being sprayed.

"Your father said he saw a skunk last week," Mom said. "That's probably the same one. But, that was very good thinking on your part to keep your brother from getting sprayed."

I took the ice cream from the freezer, scooped out a blob, and put it in a bowl. Then, I got the peanut butter from the cupboard and plopped a big wad of it on top of the ice cream. Cole was going to think he'd died and gone to heaven. It was his favorite treat in the whole world.

Then, I remembered my hairbrush. I'd left it on the picnic table.

"Be right back," I said to Mom. "I left my brush outside."

"Things are always found in the last place you look," Mom said.

I rolled my eyes, pulled the sliding glass door open, and slipped outside.

The sun had set, and there was only a faint, orange glow in the west, like lava in the sky, drifting away. The smell of wood smoke had faded a little, and the cool night air tickled my nostrils. The grass beneath my bare feet was cold, and my skin broke out in gooseflesh. It wouldn't be long before winter came, and I would have to wear shoes or boots when I went outside.

I reached the picnic table, picked up my hairbrush, and was about to return to the house.

That's when I heard a noise.

It was just a rustling of leaves, very soft and quiet. The skunk was still around, I was sure, and I was once again glad that Cole hadn't been sprayed.

I peered into the dark back yard, looking for the creature, but it was impossible to see.

No matter. It was just a skunk. No big deal. You see one skunk, you've seen them all.

The noise came again, louder this time. I heard what sounded like a growl.

Weird, I thought. *Skunks don't growl.*

And then, I *did* see something.

Not a skunk.

Not even the shape of a skunk.

In fact, I had no idea exactly what I saw—not at the moment, anyway.

At the back of our yard, in the dark of the new night, were two glowing, red sparks.

Eyes, burning like hot coins.

Staring.

At *me*.

Something horrible was in our back yard, watching me at that very moment!

3

Gripped by fear, I could do nothing but stare at the two sinister red eyes glaring back at me in the dark. I wanted to shout, to scream for help, but it felt like iron claws had wrapped themselves around my body, squeezing the air from my lungs. I couldn't even breathe.

What is that thing? I wondered. *And why are his eyes glowing?*

I'd never seen anything like it before. I was sure it was an animal of some sort, but what kind? It was two big to be a skunk, as the eyes were too big and too far off the ground. I wondered if it might be a dog, but I'd never seen a dog with glowing red eyes before.

Somehow, I found the courage to move. I took a step backward, then another, and another. At the far end of the yard, the red eyes remained where they were, motionless, boring into me like laser beams.

When I reached the sliding glass door I pulled it open, darted inside, and slammed it closed. I let out a huge sigh of relief.

The noise from the slamming door caught Mom by surprise, and she looked up.

"Erica," she said. "I've told you not to slam the sliding glass door."

She must have noticed the look on my face, because she looked at me curiously. "What's wrong?" she asked.

"There's something out there!" I replied. "Something with red eyes! I saw it! It's in the back yard, by the trees!"

Mom put down the mixing bowl she was holding and walked toward me. She flipped on the outside porch light peered out the sliding glass window.

"I don't see anything," she said.

The porch light lit up the back yard, giving it a cool, lemony glow. The shadow cast by the picnic table looked like a monster, stretching out over the grass to become one with the darkness.

But there was no sign of the glowing red eyes.

"I'm telling you," I said, "I saw something. There was something there. I don't know what it was, but it had red eyes. It was watching me."

"I'm sure it was probably just a dog," Mom said. "I hope he doesn't tangle with that skunk."

Mom was probably right. It probably *was* a dog. Still, we don't see many stray dogs around our neighborhood. Some of the people on our block have dogs, but they keep them in their own yards and they don't roam loose.

No matter. I was safe inside. Whatever I saw, it was *out there.* I had no reason to be afraid.

Not *yet,* anyway.

But soon.

Soon, I would find that I had good reason to be afraid . . . and it all started later that night, at exactly two o'clock in the morning when I was awakened by something very, very strange . . . .

4

Later that night:

I awoke in bed with a book on my chest. I'd fallen asleep reading. It was a book about a kid that was a wimp, and it was really good.

The light beside my bed was still on. I put the book on my night stand, clicked off the light, and pulled the covers up to my neck. I closed my eyes, and, after a few minutes, began to drift back to sleep.

A noise outside jolted me awake.

A squealing, laughing sound.

A howl.

I sat up in bed. The howl came again, and I knew what it was.

A coyote. Maybe a couple of them.

We hear them once in a while, usually late at night. Sometimes, we see them. Not very often, though. They like to come out at night, so we don't see them during the day. Last year, one was struck and killed by a car not far from our house.

The howl came again, closer this time. In fact, it sounded like it might be coming from our front yard, or in the street.

I scrambled from my bed and tiptoed to the window. Outside, the streetlight gave off a salty blue light, illuminating our yard and the street. I could see our neighbor's homes and cars parked in driveways.

And I saw something move.

Just a shadow, near a tree in our neighbor's yard. I watched for a moment, until it moved again.

Then, the animal strode out into the light. I was right! It *was* a coyote! It was about two feet tall, skinny, and long. I couldn't tell what color he was, because it was too dark, even in the glow of the streetlight.

While I watched, the animal sauntered across our front yard. He didn't appear to be in any hurry, either, and I was sure that he wasn't afraid of anything. After all: he was a creature of the night. At night, this was his territory. While other animals slept, he was out hunting for food.

Suddenly, the animal stopped. He turned his head and looked right at me. I hadn't made a move or done anything to draw his attention . . . but he saw me. He was watching me. Just like—

And that's when his eyes began to glow red, just like the animal I'd seen in the back yard!

5

That's what I saw in the back yard earlier tonight! I thought. *He has the same, glowing red eyes!*

I watched the creature watch me. He didn't come any closer; rather, he remained standing in the yard, his head low, staring.

How can an animal have eyes that glow? I wondered. It didn't seem possible. The coyote's eyes were bright red, glowing like flashlights. I've never heard of any animal being able to do that.

A movement across the street caught my

attention, and I flinched. Another coyote appeared, strolling across the street to meet up with the one in our yard. Now, both of them were staring at me. Both of them had bizarre, glowing red eyes.

In the distance, I heard another coyote howl. My window was closed, so I couldn't hear very well, but it was a howl, all right. The sound caught the attention of the two coyotes in the front yard. They looked away for a moment before returning their gaze to me.

This is just plain freaky, I thought, and I was glad I was inside. I'd never heard of coyotes bothering humans before, but something told me these weren't ordinary coyotes. There was something about these creatures that wasn't right, especially with the way they stared at me with their glowing eyes.

The strange animals watched me for another few minutes. Then, as if given some unseen signal, both of them turned and walked away, slinking off into the night, vanishing into the shadows.

Still, I remained at the window, watching, wondering if I would see them again. Wondering what they *really* were, where they came from. I decided I would tell Mom and Dad about them in the morning.

Maybe Dad would know why their eyes glowed. Maybe some coyotes have the ability to do that.

But right then, I was tired. I climbed back into bed, pulled the covers up to my chin, and fell asleep.

In the morning, I was awakened by the squawk of the television set. The volume was blaring. Cole is always the first one up at our house. He goes straight into the living room, turns on the television, plants himself on the floor, and watches cartoons. He'd sit there all day if he could, but Mom and Dad won't let him.

I climbed out of bed, stretched, and looked at myself in the mirror. My blonde hair was tangled and messy and my nightgown was wrinkled. I was glad my friends at school didn't see me like that!

And I'd forgotten all about the strange episode the night before with the two coyotes and their glowing red eyes. In fact, I didn't even think about them again . . . until I walked into the kitchen. I had just reached into the cupboard and pulled out a box of corn flakes, when I glanced into the back yard and saw something so horrifying that I dropped the cereal box. The top opened and corn flakes fell like snow on the floor at my feet. I hardly noticed.

Outside, in the back yard near the picnic table, was a dead cat.

It had been torn to shreds!

ABOUT THE AUTHOR

Johnathan Rand has authored more than 90 books since the year 2000, with well over 5 million copies in print. His series include the incredibly popular **AMERICAN CHILLERS, MICHIGAN CHILLERS, FREDDIE FERNORTNER, FEARLESS FIRST GRADER,** and **THE ADVENTURE CLUB.** He's also co-authored a novel for teens (with Christopher Knight) entitled PANDEMIA. When not traveling, Rand lives in northern Michigan with his wife and three dogs. He is also the only author in the world to have a store that sells only his works: CHILLERMANIA is located in Indian River, Michigan and is open year round. Johnathan Rand is not always at the store, but he has been known to drop by frequently. Find out more at:

www.americanchillers.com

Johnathan Rand travels internationally for school visits and book signings! For booking information, call:

1 (231) 238-0338!

www.americanchillers.com

JOIN THE FREE AMERICAN CHILLERS FAN CLUB

It's easy to join . . . and best of all, it's FREE!
Find out more today by visiting:

WWW.AMERICANCHILLERS.COM

And don't forget to browse the on-line
superstore, where you can order books, hats,
shirts, and lots more cool stuff!

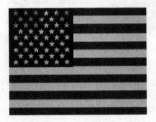

USA